Maggie's Miracle

ALSO AVAILABLE IN BEELER LARGE PRINT BY
KAREN KINGSBURY

Gideon's Gift

Maggie's Miracle

Karen Kingsbury

BEELER LARGE PRINT
Rollinsford, New Hampshire, 2004

Library of Congress Cataloging-in-Publication Data

Kingsbury, Karen.
     Maggie's miracle / Karen Kingsbury.
       p.   cm.
     ISBN 1-57490-560-0 (acid-free paper)
     1. Single mothers—Fiction. 2. Father figures—Fiction. 3. Portland (Or.)—Fiction. 4. Women lawyers—Fiction. 5. Widows—Fiction. 6. Large type books. I. Title.

PS3561.I4873M34 2004
813'.54—dc22   2004001795

Published in Large Print by arrangement with
R-Warner, Warner Books,
an AOL Time Warner Book Group.

BEELER LARGE PRINT
is published by
Thomas T. Beeler, *Publisher*
Post Office Box 310
Rollinsford, New Hampshire 03869-0310

Typeset in 16 point Times New Roman type.
Sewn and bound on acid-free paper by
Sheridan Books in Chelsea, Michigan

dedicated to...

Donald, my forever prince
Kelsey, my beautiful laughter
Tyler, my favorite song
Sean, my indefinable joy
Josh, my gentle giant
EJ, my chosen one
Austin, my miracle boy

And to God Almighty, the author of life,
who has–for now–blessed me with these.

Prologue

THE LETTER WAS HIS BEST IDEA YET.

Jordan Wright had already talked to God about getting his wish, and so far nothing had happened. But a letter . . . a letter would definitely get God's attention. Not the crayoned pictures he liked to send Grandpa in California. But a real letter. On his mom's fancy paper with his best spelling and slow hands, so his a's and e's would sit straight on the line the way a second grader's a's and e's should.

That way, God would read it for sure.

Grandma Terri was watching her yucky grown-up show on TV. People kissing and crying and yelling at each other. Every day his grandma picked him up from St. Andrews, brought him home to their Upper East Side apartment in Manhattan, got him a snack, and put in the video of her grown-up show. Jordan could make his own milk shakes or accidentally color on the walls or jump on his bed for an hour when Grandma watched her grown-up show. As long as he wasn't too loud, she didn't notice anything.

"This is my time, Jordan," she'd tell him, and her eyes would get that in-charge kind of look. "Keep yourself busy."

But when the show was over she'd find him and make a loud, huffy sound. "Jordan," she'd say, "what are you into now? Why can't you read quietly like other children?" Her voice would be slow and tired, and Jordan wouldn't know what to do next.

She never yelled at him or sent him to his room, but one thing was sure. She didn't like baby-sitting him because yesterday Jordan heard her tell his mom that.

"I can't handle the boy forever, Megan. It's been two years since George died. You need a nanny." She did a different kind of breathy noise. "The boy's wearing me out."

Jordan had been in his room listening. He felt bad because maybe it was his fault his grandma couldn't handle him. But then he heard his mom say, "I can't handle him, either, so that makes two of us."

After that Jordan felt too sick to eat dinner.

Ever since then he'd known it was time. He had to do whatever it took to get God's attention because if he didn't get his wish pretty soon, well, maybe his mom and his grandma might not like him anymore.

It wasn't that he tried to get into trouble. But sometimes it was boring looking for things to do, and he'd get curious and wonder what would happen if he made a milk shake with ice cubes. But how was he supposed to know the milk-shake maker had a lid? And using paper and a red crayon to trace the tiger on the wall calendar probably wasn't a good idea in the first place, because of course sometimes crayons slip.

He took the last swallow from his milk and waited until the cookie crumbs slid down the glass into his mouth. Cookies were the best snack of all. He set the cup on the counter, climbed off the barstool, and walked with tiptoe feet into his mom's office. He wasn't allowed in there except if his mom was working on her lawyer stuff and he had to ask her a serious question.

But she'd understand today because a letter to God

2

was very serious business.

The room was big and clean and full of wood stuff. His mom was the kind of lawyer who put bad guys in jail. That's why sometimes she had to work late at night and on Sundays. Jordan pulled open a drawer near his mother's computer and took out two pieces of paper and two envelopes. In case he messed up and had to start over. Then he snuck real quiet out the door, down the hall, and into his room. He had a desk and pencils in there, only he never used them because second graders at St. Andrews didn't get homework till after Christmas.

One time he asked his mommy what would happen if he couldn't do the homework when he got it, what if the stuff he had to do was too hard.

"It won't be too hard, Jordan." His mother's eyebrows had lifted up the way they did when she didn't want any more questions.

"Are you sure?"

"Yes, I'm completely sure."

"How come?"

"Because, Jordan, I've been through second grade and I know all the answers. If you have trouble, I'll help you."

His heart felt a little less scared after that. Not every second grader's mommy had all the answers. If she knew everything, then he could never really get in too much trouble with his homework, and that was a good thing because Christmas wasn't too far away.

He sat down at his desk, took a pencil from the box, and spread out the piece of paper. The white space looked very empty. Jordan stared at it for a long time. If God was going to read the letter, it had to be his best work ever. Big words would be a good thing. He worked himself a little taller in the chair, sucked in a long breath through his teeth, and began to write.

Dear God, my name is Jordan Wright and I am 8 years old. I hav somthing to ask you. I tride to ask you befor but I think you wer bizy. So I am riting you a letter insted.

Jordan's hand hurt by the time he finished, and he could hear music playing on Grandma's grown-up show. That meant it was almost done, and any minute Grandma would come looking for him. He quickly folded the letter in half, ran his finger along the edge, and folded it again. Then he stuck it in the envelope and licked the lid shut. With careful fingers he wrote "God" across the front, then his pencil moved down a bit and froze. He'd forgotten something.

He didn't know God's address.

His heart felt extra jumpy. God lived in heaven, so that had to be part of it. But what about the numbers? Jordan could hear footsteps coming closer. He didn't want Grandma to see the letter. She might want to read it, and that would ruin everything because it was a secret. Just between him and God. He looked around his room and saw his backpack near his bed. He ran fast to it and slipped the letter inside. He could give it to his mother on the way to school tomorrow. She would know God's address.

She knew everything.

Chapter One

MEGAN WRIGHT TUCKED HER BLOUSE into her navy skirt as she rounded the corner into the kitchen. Her biggest opening argument of the month was in less than an hour. "Let's go, Jordan. Two minutes."

"Just a sec."

"Not just a sec." She blew at a wisp of hair as she grabbed a cold piece of toast from the kitchen counter. These were the times she missed George more than any other because the morning routine had been his deal. As long as he was at work by eight-thirty he'd been happy. But she had briefings and depositions that started earlier than that.

"*Now*, Jordan. I have a hearing today."

She poured two glasses of orange juice, snatched one and spun toward the vitamin cupboard. Two C's, one A, one E, a B-complex, a CoQ_{10}, and two garlics. She popped the pills into her mouth and swallowed them with a single swig of juice. George had been more than twenty years older than her, a man she respected and tried to love. But the fortress surrounding George's deepest emotions was unyielding stone and razor wire, and in his presence, Megan never felt like more than an amicable business partner. When the love she'd dreamed of never materialized, Megan allowed herself to become like him. Married to her job.

Neither of them had figured Jordan into the plans.

But surprise gave way to possibility, and for a time Megan believed that maybe George would come around, spend less time at work, and get caught up in fatherhood. They would have quiet moments together, watching their baby sleep and dreaming of his future. Laughter and passion would finally find them, and her life would be all she'd ever hoped it to be. But the dream never quite materialized. George was nearly fifty by then, and thrilled with the idea of a son, a child to carry on his name, but he was as distant as ever with Megan.

"You treat me like part of the furniture, George." Megan whispered the words to him one night after they climbed into bed. "Don't you want more?"

His eyes had been steely cold. "You have all you could ever want, Megan. Don't ask more of me than I can give."

George had been a bond trader, a financial wizard with a spacious office in Midtown. For two weeks straight he'd complained about a stiff neck, but neither of them saw the signs. When his secretary found him that October morning, arms spread across his desk, his head resting on a pile of client files, she'd thought he was merely resting. An hour later a client call came in and she tried to wake him. Her scream brought most of the office staff and fifteen minutes later paramedics gave them the truth.

He was dead, the victim of a massive coronary.

Megan lifted the juice to her lips once more and downed it in four swallows. It had been two years now. Her grieving period had lasted only a few months. The two of them had never loved the way Megan had hoped, the way she'd once, a long time ago, believed possible. She and George were business partners, friends who ran

6

a common household. She missed George in a functionary sense—especially on mornings like this—but he'd taken none of her heart with him when he died.

The problem was Jordan.

The boy was the one person George had truly loved, and what little free time and sparse emotions he was able to give had been completely reserved for their only child. Megan never admitted it, but more than once she'd found herself feeling jealous of George's love for Jordan. Because it was a love he'd never had for her. When George died, Jordan was devastated. In the two years since his death, the level of Jordan's behavior in school and at home had plummeted.

Grief and anger, his doctor had called it. A passing phase. Megan and Jordan met with a counselor after George's death, but the sessions were costly and time-consuming, and Megan didn't notice any improvement in Jordan's behavior. She'd asked her doctor about medication for the boy. Ritalin or one of the other drugs kids were using.

"Let's wait." The pediatrician had angled his head thoughtfully. "I still think his behavior is related to the loss of his father."

That was three months ago, and Megan was tired of waiting.

Her mother had lived with them since just after George's death, an arrangement Megan had thought would be best for all of them. Her mom had retired from teaching in Florida that year and lived on a limited income. They could share expenses, and her mother could help her with Jordan after school and on the weekends. But Jordan was too much for her mother, especially now that the weather was cooler and they were inside more.

She set the juice glass in the dishwasher. "Jordan!"

Her son's tennis shoes sounded on the hardwood hallway as he ran into view. "Sorry, Mom."

Megan looked at the boy and felt her patience waning. "Jordan, orange and green?"

"Miss Hanson says October is orange month."

"Miss Hanson isn't your mother." Megan pointed down the hallway. "Find something that matches, and do it now. We have to go."

"Okay." Jordan ran back down the hall, his steps a bit slower this time.

Megan glanced at the clock on the microwave oven. 7:16 a.m. They'd have to catch every green light along Madison Avenue to make it on time. She darted into her bathroom, brushed her teeth, and checked her look. Trim and professional, dark hair swept into a conservative knot, makeup applied just so. She still turned heads, but not because she was pretty.

Because she was powerful.

At thirty-two she was one of the youngest prosecutors in the borough, and she had no intention of getting sidetracked. Not until the D.A.'s office was hers alone. That hadn't been her goal before George's heart attack, but now—now that she was their single source of income, things would always be tight if she didn't keep climbing.

"Jordan . . ." She grabbed her leather jacket and flung her bag over her shoulder. "Now!"

He was waiting for her near the door. "Beat ya!"

His crooked grin caught her off guard, and for half a second she smiled. "Very funny."

"Big hearing?" Jordan opened the door for her.

Megan shut and locked it. "The biggest."

They hurried down the stairs and out onto the street.

It was raining, and Megan hailed the first cab she saw. "Get in, Jordan. Hurry."

He tossed his backpack in and slid over. She didn't have the door shut before she said, "Fifth and 102nd. Fast."

The routine was the same every morning, but sometimes—days like today—they had less room for error. They were a block away from school when Jordan pulled something from his backpack and stuck it in Megan's bag. "Hey, Mom. Could you mail this? Please?"

Megan jerked a folder from her purse and opened it. The hearing notes were in there somewhere. She'd stayed up until after midnight studying them, but she wouldn't be prepared without going over them one more time.

"Mom?"

The folder settled on Megan's lap and she looked at Jordan. "What is it, honey? Mommy's busy with her court notes."

"I'm sorry." His eyes fell to his hands for a moment. "I put something in your bag."

"Right . . ." Megan concentrated. What had the boy said? Something about the mail? "What was it again?"

Jordan reached into her bag and lifted a white envelope from the side pocket. "It's a letter. Could you put the 'dress on it and mail it this morning? It's important."

"*Address.*" Megan raised her eyebrows at him. Whatever they taught kids at St. Andrews, it wasn't enough. Her son's academic abilities were nowhere near Megan's expectations for an eight-year-old child. Yes, he could hit a ball over the fence and throw it to home plate. But that wouldn't help him get into college. She

9

patted his cheek. "The word is *address*. Not 'dress."

"Address." Jordan didn't skip a beat. "Could ya, Mom? Please?"

She dropped her eyes back to the folder and lifted it closer to her face. "Sure, yes." She cast him a brief smile. "Definitely." The letter was probably for his grandpa Howard in California. But usually he addressed them.

The cab rumbled along, inching its way through a sea of early-morning yellow, but Megan barely noticed as she studied her notes. Getting a conviction on the case was a sure thing. The defendant was a nineteen-year-old up for murder one, the ringleader of a gang of teens who'd spent a week that past summer lying in wait for late-night female victims in Central Park. In each case, the young men studied their prey for days, watching them enough to know their walking pattern, the direction they came from, and what time of night.

At an opportune moment, they'd grab the victim, strangle her with fishing wire, and rob her clean. They dumped the bodies in the brush and made their escape through back trails out to the street. The first two times, the gang pulled off their deed without a hitch. The third time, an off-duty police officer happened by and heard someone struggling in the bushes. He darted off the path into the bramble, and a gun battle ensued. The victim escaped with bruises on her neck, but the police officer and one of the gang members were killed in the fight.

Megan wanted the death penalty.

The cab jarred to a stop. "St. Andrews." The cabbie put the car in park and didn't turn around.

"We're here, honey." Megan leaned over and gave Jordan a peck on his cheek. "Get your bag."

Jordan grabbed his backpack, climbed out of the cab,

10

and looked back at her. "Don't forget, okay?"

Megan's mind was blank. "Forget what?"

"Mom!" Jordan's shoulders slumped some. "My letter. Don't forget to mail my letter."

"Right . . . sorry." Megan gave a firm nod of her head. "I won't forget."

"Promise?"

Something desperate shone in his little-boy eyes, and Megan felt as if she were seeing him for the first time that morning. He was a great kid, really, and she loved him in a way that sometimes scared her. But then why didn't she spend more time with him? She had no answers for herself, and suddenly she needed to hug him more than she needed air. Even if she missed her hearing.

She slid out of the car and went to him, pulling him into her arms and ignoring the surprise in his eyes. Her answer was quiet, whispered against the top of his head. "Promise." For the briefest moment she savored the way he smelled, the way he felt in her arms—like a little boy again. "Have a good day, okay?"

His arms tightened some, and he pressed his face against her. "I'm sorry I'm so much trouble."

Megan shot a quick look at the cabbie. "You're not so much trouble, honey. We'll figure everything out somehow." She glanced at her watch. "Okay, buddy. Mom can't be late. Love you."

"Love you." Jordan gave her one last look, then darted up the sidewalk to St. Andrews. Megan climbed back into the cab and watched until he was safely through the front door, then she turned to the driver and raised her voice a notch. "Supreme Court on Centre." She straightened her notes and slipped them back in the folder. "Fast."

* * *

It was nightfall before Megan had a chance to grab a cup of coffee, sit down, and go over the cases she'd worked on that day. The hearing had gone brilliantly. The jury—made up of married women and retired men—was bound to be more conservative than most in Manhattan, and her opening remarks had been right on. By the time she sat down, half the jurors were nodding in agreement. The trial would take two weeks of formalities, and she'd have her conviction.

She liked to call Jordan after school, but the morning hearing had blended into an afternoon briefing and two late depositions. Now it was seven o'clock, and she still hadn't gone over her files, five of them spread out across her desk. One at a time she worked her way through each document, checking the facts, going over witness lists, looking for loopholes. Trying to think like a defense attorney in case some small detail had slipped her mind. By seven-thirty she was convinced none had.

She was loading the files into a cabinet when the phone on her desk rang. Megan grabbed the receiver and kept filing. "Hello?"

"Megan, I can't take it. The boy made a racetrack in the bathroom and flushed a Mustang down the toilet. We have an inch of water on the floor, and the supe's on his way up because Mrs. Paisley in 204 has a wet ceiling." Her mother paused only long enough to refuel. "I fixed chicken for dinner, but by then he didn't want to eat, so I sent him to his room to read. He's been crying for the past half hour."

Megan shut the file drawer and fell back into her chair. "A wet ceiling? Mom . . . how long was it flooded?"

"Not long, and don't have that tone with me."

"You were watching your soap, weren't you? No wonder he was playing in the toilet."

"Megan, the boy's crying. Come home. We'll talk about it here."

Traffic was a nightmare, and Megan used the time to think about her life. Tears were nothing new for Jordan, not lately. She thought about her options, but none of them brought her peace. Her mother was right, the boy needed a friend—someone to take walks with and play sports with. But where would she find someone like that?

A fragment of a conversation played in Megan's mind. A couple had been talking in the halls outside Megan's office.

"Child support is fine, but he needs more than that." The woman kept her voice to a low hiss.

"It's not my problem. I'm writing the checks; that's all the court asked me to do."

"We wouldn't be here if you spent even a few days a month with him, can't you see that? Kids need more than food and a roof over their heads."

Megan stared out the window of the cab at the dark, wet streets of New York City. *More than food and a roof over their heads* . . . The words echoed in the most solitary part of her heart, the part she'd closed off the spring of her thirteenth year.

That was the problem with Jordan, of course. He was lonely, left with only a tired old woman far too often. The truth made Megan's eyes sting and it roughed up the surface of her perfect plans. She'd have time for Jordan later, when she made a name for herself as a prosecutor, when she was making big money and able to choose her hours. Wasn't that what she always told herself? For now, Jordan had to know she loved him.

She told him all the time.

It took Megan half an hour to get home. She rarely felt tired after a full day in court; exhilarated but not tired. Today, though, she wanted only to bypass the situation with Jordan and go straight to bed. The three flights of stairs felt like five, and Jordan met her at the door.

"Did you do it?"

Megan locked eyes with him as she walked in and closed the door behind her. "Do what?"

"Mail the letter." Hope shone in his expression. "Did you?"

Her heart skipped a beat, and she resisted the urge to blink. "Of course."

"Really? You found the address?"

The lie came easier the second time. She brushed at a wisp of his hair and kissed his forehead. "Definitely."

Jordan flung his arms around her. "Thanks, Mom . . . you're the best."

Guilt found its way to her throat and put down roots. "Enough about that." She swallowed hard and pulled back. "What happened in the bathroom?"

It was an hour later before they got through the story and she tucked him into bed. By then her mother was asleep, and finally Megan took her bag and retreated to her bedroom. The letter was still tucked inside. As she pulled it out her heart stumbled. Jordan had scribbled just one word across the front of the envelope:

God.

Suddenly she remembered. Jordan had asked her to address it before dropping it in the mail. Megan closed her eyes, clutched the letter to her heart, and exhaled hard. Then, afraid of what she'd find, she dropped to her bed and opened it. Inside was a single page, filled with Jordan's neatest handwriting.

Megan narrowed her eyes and began to read.

Dear God, my name is Jordan Wright and I am 8 years old. I hav somthing to ask you. I tride to ask you befor but I think you wer bizy. So I am riting you a letter insted.

A sad, aching sort of pain ignited in the basement of Megan's soul, the place where she had assigned all feelings about God and prayers and miracles. Jordan had said it perfectly. God had always been too busy to hear the prayers of a lonely, forgotten woman, and now He was too busy for her son. She gritted her teeth and kept reading.

I hav a wish to ask you abot, and here it is: Plese God, send me a Daddy. My daddy died wen his heart stopped pumping, and now its just my mom and gramma and me.

Tears filled Megan's eyes and made the words blurry. She blinked and forced herself to continue.

My frend Keith has a daddy who plays baseball with him and takes him on Saterday trips to the park and helps him with his plusses and minuses evry day after scool. Mommy is too bizy to do that stuff, so plese God, plese send me a Daddy like that. Chrismas would be a good time. Thank you very much. Love, Jordan.

Megan wiped her tears. She read the letter again and again, and finally a fourth time as the sobs welled within her. Deep, gut-wrenching sobs of the type she hadn't allowed herself since she was a little girl. She could give Jordan everything he needed, but never the one thing he wanted. A daddy—a man to play with him and love him and call him his own.

And the fact grieved her as it hadn't since George died.

Megan slipped the letter back inside the envelope and eased it under her pillow. Then, with her work clothes still on, she lay down, slid beneath the comforter, and covered her face with her hands. Suddenly she was thirteen again, alone on the sandy shores of Lake Tahoe, devastated by her own losses and desperate for answers.

The boy had been fifteen, tall and wiry with sun-drenched hair and freckles, and they met each other near the water every day for a week. What was his name? Kade something? The memory was dimmer than it had once been, and she could barely picture his face. But Maggie had never forgotten something the boy told her that summer.

Hold out for real love, Maggie, because real love never fails.

Megan had gazed out across the chilly lake and shook her head. It would take a miracle for that kind of love, she'd told him. Nothing short of a miracle.

"Then that," the boy had said as he grinned at her, "is what I'll pray for. A miracle for Maggie."

Megan rolled onto her side and let the full brunt of the sobs come. For years she'd held on to the boy's definition of love—a love that would never fail. But the boy on the beach had been wrong. Love—whatever love was—certainly failed. And miracles? Well, they didn't happen for her, and they certainly weren't about to happen for Jordan.

The sooner he understood that, the better off he'd be.

Chapter Two

YEAR-ROUND, Saturday mornings were busy at Casey's Corner in Midtown Manhattan. The smell of hot blueberry pancakes and sizzling bacon drenched the air, while the clamor of clattering trays and a dozen conversations served as a backdrop for customers lined up at the door. The café was a hot spot for tourists from Texas to Tokyo and extremely popular among Midtown's business elite. With a menu that was "healthy eclectic," ripe avocado and alfalfa sprout sandwiches were served up alongside a half dozen styles of homemade cheesecake. The food was fresh and fast, and the atmosphere as diverse and dynamic as New York City itself. In the six years since Casey Cummins opened the café, it had practically become a local landmark.

One of the regulars was telling him a joke, and Casey had to remind himself to laugh. His mind was a million miles away, stranded on an island of memories and secrets he would share with no one.

Especially today.

Most days, Casey jogged to work. He wore his trademark blue nylon sweats and white Nikes, same as always, so that when the morning was behind him he could run the twenty blocks through Central Park back to his apartment. His routine was the same as it had always been, but these days Casey logged more miles and rarely ran the straight path to his front door. Not because he needed the exercise, but because he wanted to be anywhere but back at the lonely set of walls he called home.

It was the third Saturday in October, and Casey easily drifted from one conversation to another as he made the rounds. "Joey . . . how's the new job at the bank?" or "Hey, Mrs. Jackson, another Saturday closer to Christmas," or "Marvin, my man, how 'bout those Nets? Jason Kidd'll tear 'em up this season."

Hours passed, and Casey kept himself in the moment. Never mind that his thoughts were somewhere else, the café routine was as familiar as putting one foot in front of the other. Even on a day like this.

The crowd began thinning around noon, and Casey found a seat at the counter. "Long morning, Billy-G."

The old black chef peered out from his position in front of the kitchen stove. "Okay . . ." He studied Casey for a moment. "Give it up."

Casey blinked and kept his gaze on the man's face. Billy Gaynor was a quiet family man from Nigeria who'd worked for Casey since the café opened. Billy's culinary magic was as much a part of the success of Casey's Corner as the quirky New York street signs and Broadway memorabilia that hung on the hand-painted walls. Casey and Billy-G were colleagues and friends— even more so since Amy died. They were both widowers now, and despite the thirty years between them, there was no one Casey would rather spend an hour with.

Billy-G was waiting, and Casey grabbed a nearby pitcher, poured himself a cup of coffee, and took a slow drink.

"Yes, sir." Casey peered over the top of his steaming mug. "Another great Saturday morning in the Big

Apple, eh Billy-G."

His friend's eyebrows forged a slow path through the thick skin that made up his forehead. "Ya ain't fooling me, Casey." He lumbered around the corner and leaned against the counter opposite Casey. "Ya gotta talk about it." Customers still filled most of the seats, so Billy-G kept his voice low. "You can't fake it with me, Casey. I already know."

Casey set down his coffee and lowered his chin. He thought about smiling again, but changed his mind. "What ya know, Billy-G?"

"It's your anniversary." The man leaned closer. "One month after mine, remember?"

A brief burning nipped at Casey's eyes. "That." He sniffed hard and sat up straighter on the stool. "No big deal, Billy-G. Life moves on."

"Yes." The old man leaned against the counter, his eyes still locked on Casey's. "But only a fool would forget a girl like Amy." He hesitated and took a step back toward the kitchen. "And you ain't no fool."

"Yeah, well . . ." Casey narrowed his eyes some and sucked in a quick breath. He set down his cup and gave the counter a light slap. "Time for my jog."

Billy-G stopped and leveled his gaze at Casey once more. "I'm here. Anytime you wanna talk, I'm here."

"Thanks." Casey glanced over his shoulder and mentally mapped out a course for the door. His throat was thick, and memories were drawing close to the surface. Some days he could talk about Amy for hours and never feel the tears. Times like those he liked nothing more than to hang out with Billy-G after closing time and talk about a thousand yesterdays. But not today.

He flashed a smile at Billy-G. "See ya tomorrow."

The pavement felt like ice beneath his feet, and Casey ran faster than usual. Some of the regulars had waved him down, hoping for a conversation or a laugh, but he couldn't pretend for another minute. Billy-G was right.

Casey Cummins was no fool, and today he could keep up the happy-guy act only for so long. It was his eighth wedding anniversary, and if Amy and the baby had lived, they would've spent the day together, celebrating life and love and cherishing that special something they'd had between them, the kind of love so few people shared.

He headed north on Broadway and cut across the street toward Central Park. The thing of it was, no one wanted to hear about his loss. Not really. People had their own tragedies, lost jobs and children in the Armed Forces, broken relationships and bankruptcies. At Casey's Corner everyone wanted a sympathetic ear, and he made it his job to listen.

But rarely did he talk.

Casey slowed his pace some and headed into the park on a paved path. He'd heard people question God after a tragedy, wondering how a loving Creator could allow a world filled with devastation and loss. Some of his customers were so angry with God after September 11, they'd stopped believing.

Casey didn't feel that way at all.

Bad things happened in the world, it was that simple. A fifteen-year-old rape victim, the mother of a toddler killed by a drunk driver, the wife of a police officer shot in the line of duty—each of them had their own September 11, a day when they'd been forced to realize that without faith, life didn't make sense.

Not a single minute of it.

Casey's had happened a week after the terrorist attacks, on September 18. That was the day Amy went into labor and began bleeding. He rushed her to Mount Sinai Hospital, and even after the doctors ushered him into a private waiting room, Casey thought Amy and the baby were going to be fine. It wasn't until almost an hour later, when a weary doctor shuffled up to Casey, that he realized something was wrong.

"We lost them both, Mr. Cummins." The doctor had tears in his eyes. "I'm sorry."

Amy had begun hemorrhaging when she went into labor. The blood loss was too much, and there'd been no way to save either of them.

Casey was breathing harder now. He rounded a corner and saw the familiar green and tan plastic play equipment and the giant slide to the right. The East Meadow play area wasn't the largest or most popular in Central Park, but it was the place where Casey and Amy had come after they'd moved to New York. Normally, he would run past the area with only a quick glance and a flash of memories. Past the worn-out bench anchored near the back by the big slide, past the place where he had given Amy a ring, the place where she'd told him she was going to have a baby. The quiet spot where they'd held each other and wept once the dust settled after the collapse of the Twin Towers.

He slowed his steps and came to a stop, his sides heaving. The place, the bench, was a graveyard of memories, and most days he was better off not to stop.

But today . . .

Today, there was suddenly nowhere else he wanted to be.

A chill hung in the air, and the bushes rustled with a strong fall breeze. Casey gripped his knees and bent

21

over, waiting for his lungs to fill. After a few seconds, he straightened and linked his hands behind his head. For half a minute he moved his feet in small circles, until his breathing was normal again. A dozen children were scattered amid the swings and slides, and not far away their parents stood in clusters or sat on other benches, chatting and sometimes yelling out at the little ones, warning them not to walk in front of swings or promising to play with them in a few minutes.

The voices faded, and Casey headed toward the back of the play area. Their bench was empty, like always. It was smaller, older than the others, and partially hidden by an overgrown bush. Only half the play equipment could be seen from that bench, so most of the parents didn't bother with it.

He sat down and stretched out his legs. The ground was damp, carpeted with a layer of month-old fallen leaves. Casey kicked at a dark, wet clump and crossed his feet.

Eight years.

If Amy had lived they would've been close to celebrating a decade together. He let his head fall back a few inches and stared into the gray. *Come on, let me see her . . . just once.* He narrowed his eyes, willing himself to look beyond the clouds to the place where Amy still lived, still loved him and waited for him.

But all he could see was the swirl of late-autumn sky, and his heart settled deeper in his chest. He closed his eyes.

The pain is worse now than ever. I— He held his breath, determined to keep his emotions at bay. *I miss her so much.*

His eyes opened, and a robin caught his attention. It hopped along the sidewalk a few feet away, studying the ground, pecking at it. Then it stopped and tilted its head toward the trees, and in a rush of motion, flapped its wings and lifted into the air.

Casey watched until it disappeared. If Amy were here, she'd slip her arm around his shoulders and tell him to learn a thing or two from the robin. What good ever came from muddling around on the ground? It had been two years and Amy would've wanted him to fly again. Live again . . . love again. Amy, with her wheat-colored blonde hair and light brown eyes, her easy laugh and tender heart. The unaffected way she said exactly what was on her mind.

Come on, Casey . . . He could almost hear her, see the sparks flying in her eyes. *What're you going to do . . . stop breathing? Get out there and live.*

But where would he start? And with whom? And how—after loving and losing the woman of his dreams—was he supposed to fly again? So what if two years had passed. He didn't want to fly yet, didn't want to move on. Better to be alone with her memories than find someone to replace her.

The very idea made his stomach hurt.

"Jordan, not so high." A woman's voice broke the moment, and Casey's eyes followed the sound. She was a brunette, pretty in a professional sort of way, and she stood a few feet from the play equipment. "Jordan . . . did you hear me?"

Casey shifted his gaze to the big slide and saw a young boy, seven or eight years old. For a moment he looked as though he might disobey her, but then he stopped, turned around, and headed back down the ladder. Casey blinked, and he was back in the hospital room again, hearing the news about his wife and child for the first time.

23

The baby had been a boy.

The doctor had said so right after telling him the awful news. A boy who would've had Amy's eyes and Casey's sense of adventure. A boy like the one climbing on the play equipment. He would've been two years old, and he would've loved the East Meadow, where the carpet of green gave way to a view of the reservoir. Yes, this would've been his favorite place. Amy would've been by his side, holding his hand, and together they would've watched their son run and skip and jump across the play bridge.

Casey shifted his gaze, and the invisible picture disappeared. He sucked in a quick breath and slid a bit lower on the bench. Why was he letting his thoughts run wild? What good did daydreaming do him now? So what if it was their anniversary. Amy was gone—and with her every hope he'd ever had for the future. There was no hand to hold, no happy ending, and no towheaded little boy to play with.

He stood and turned around, using the back of the bench to stretch his legs behind him one at a time, loosening his arches and calves for the run home. No reason to stay another moment. The bench was nothing but a tombstone now. A tombstone marking Amy's easy grin, and a baby boy's unheard cry, and every other good thing about life and living, all of which had died on the operating table right alongside Amy and their infant son.

Chapter Three

MEGAN HAD CAUGHT GLIMPSES of the man ever since she and Jordan arrived.

The park had been Jordan's idea, the least she could do after reading his letter to God. She couldn't take the place of a father, but she loved the boy, and the letter had done nothing but underline the fact. Jordan needed more time with her, and now she would do whatever she could to be there for him. If that meant giving up a Saturday at the office, she would find another way to get the work done.

She'd been pushing Jordan on the swing, laughing at something he'd said, when the man jogged up, cooled down a bit, and sat on a bench at the far back near the big slide. Megan met his eyes only briefly as he walked past, but immediately she knew something was wrong. Megan was an attorney, after all. She could read body language and facial expressions as easily as she could read a court paper.

And she was an expert at reading eyes.

The man's were haunting, filled with the kind of private pain you saw in theater seats and restaurants and office places, a pain that was commonplace in New York City. At least in the last two years. For a moment, Megan wondered about the man's story. He looked nice enough, and the way he held himself stirred something vaguely familiar in her. For a moment she wondered. Had he lost a parent or a child? A lover, maybe. Or was he merely struggling with a rough workweek?

Ten minutes passed, and Megan considered the solitary man. Maybe she should go to him, find out why he was here and what made his eyes look that way. Maybe he wanted to talk. Megan turned her attention to Jordan and the idea passed. Crazy thoughts like that didn't flit across her mind very often. The man was obviously sitting alone for a reason, and Megan wasn't about to interrupt him.

"Time me, Mom." Jordan waved at her. His eyes danced as they hadn't in months, and Megan felt a ripple of hope. Everything would be all right. She could do this—this playtime thing. And eventually, Jordan would see that he didn't need a father, not with how much she loved him.

"Time you?" She looked at her watch. "For what?"

"See how long it takes me to run around the swings, climb the ladder, and drop down the slide, okay?"

"Okay." Megan did a salute in Jordan's direction. "Whenever you're ready."

For the longest time, the two of them played the game, and when Jordan was finally too tired to make another go at it, Megan noticed that the man was gone. Gone home to whatever family waited for him, whatever it was that caused his eyes so much sorrow.

Jordan jumped off the slide and jogged over to her. "Ready?"

"Yep." Megan pushed up the sleeves of her sweater and rose to her feet. "Ready if you are."

He walked alongside her and yawned. "That was way fun."

"*Way* fun?"

"Come on, Mom . . ." Jordan grinned at her. "You know, like really, *really* fun."

26

"Oh . . ." Megan tilted her head back and shot him a teasing look. "All right, then I *way* liked being with you today."

"Yeah . . ." The silliness faded from Jordan's eyes, and he gave her the type of adoring smile she hadn't seen for years. "Me, too."

See, Jordan, she wanted to say. *You don't need a dad.* "Wanna get lunch?"

"Don't you have to work?" Jordan stopped walking and turned to her. His mouth was open.

"Nope." She tickled him in the ribs. "I'm yours all day."

"Really?"

"Really."

Jordan jumped and raised his fist in the air the way he did when his favorite football team scored a touchdown. "Yes!"

Megan laughed, and the sound of it stuck in her heart. Like a favorite song she hadn't heard in far too long. She lowered her chin and grinned at Jordan. "Does that mean pizza or hot dogs?"

"Hot dogs near the Conservatory. Definitely." They started walking again, and this time Jordan tucked his hand in hers. "Hey, Mom . . ."

"Yes." Megan ran her thumb along the side of Jordan's hand and realized something. She'd told Jordan the truth. Spending the day with him had been wonderful and refreshing, the perfect break after a long week.

"You look pretty today."

Megan angled her head and gave a single nod in Jordan's direction. "Why, thank you, kind sir." She ran her fingers through her short dark hair. "Must be my new haircut."

"No . . ." Jordan shook his head. "It's the jeans. Mommies look nice in jeans."

The conversation veered from jeans to the zoo animals at the far end of the park to the open house at school the coming week to the one thing Megan had desperately hoped he wouldn't talk about.

The God letter.

It happened when they were twenty yards from the hot-dog vendor. Jordan let go of her hand and pivoted to a standstill. "Mom!" Concern flashed in his eyes. "You mailed my letter, right?"

Megan's heart skipped a beat. "Letter?"

Jordan knit his eyebrows together. "The one I put inside your purse. Yesterday, before school?"

"Oh, that." Megan urged herself to smile. "Of course I mailed it." She started walking again and he fell in beside her. "I already told you that."

"When did you?"

It took all of Megan's effort to spit out the lie. "Just after lunch." She kept her eyes straight ahead, moving along as though nothing were wrong.

"But you found the address?"

Megan felt two inches high. "Yes, Jordan." She pointed at the vendor. "How 'bout hot dogs and chips?"

Jordan skipped a bit in front of her and tossed a smile over his shoulder. "I knew you'd know the address for God, you know why?"

Megan ordered herself to look relaxed. "Why?"

"Because you know everything, Mom. Even God's address." He glanced ahead at the vendor. "Hot dogs are perfect."

They were in line when Megan found her voice again. "Uh . . . Jordan . . . about the letter . . ."

"Yeah?"

"What . . . what exactly did you tell God?"

Jordan lifted his shoulders twice. "I just sort of asked Him something." He squinted his eyes and looked toward the sky. The clouds had burned off, and blue patches were showing above them. "It's a secret. Between me and God."

Megan could kick herself for pushing the issue, but she'd hoped he might tell her what it held. That way she could break the news to him gently—that God wouldn't be hand-delivering a daddy anytime soon. But if Jordan wouldn't tell her what the letter said, she could hardly let on that she knew.

They moved up a bit in line, and Jordan looked at her once more. "Mom . . . are you ever gonna get married again?"

The question shot darts at Megan's soul. "No." Her answer was quick and pointed. "Not ever."

Jordan let his gaze fall to his feet, and he kicked up a bit of loose gravel. When he looked up again, his eyes were flatter than before. "How come?"

A sigh filtered through Megan's tight throat. "Because . . ." She took Jordan's hands in hers and faced him, ignoring the people in line on either side of them. "I'll never find anyone who loves me as much as you do, buddy. Okay?"

"You still believe in love, though, right?"

Megan felt his words like so many rocks. "Of course." She squeezed Jordan's hands and managed a curious smile. "Why would you ask?"

"Because one time—" Jordan hesitated. "One time I heard you tell Grandma that you didn't believe in love anymore."

"Well . . ." They were next in line, and Megan

29

couldn't let her surprise show. She would have to be more careful about what she said around the apartment. "Sometimes I get sad about Daddy being gone, and I feel that way. But not most of the time, okay?"

"Okay." He smiled at her, but the spark from earlier was gone.

They bought their hot dogs, and for the rest of the afternoon Megan grieved the fact that Jordan had heard her say such a thing about love. Worse, she grieved that what she had said was true. She didn't believe in love, not for a minute. How far had she come since that long-ago summer when—in the midst of the worst days of her life—she'd been given the gift of hope by a boy she hadn't seen before or since?

And that night as she drifted off to sleep, she didn't think about court cases or Jordan's loneliness or how a person could wake up one morning with neck pain and be dead of a coronary by noon. Rather, she allowed twenty-year-old memories to surface like seaweed, memories she'd buried long ago. And as she did, she felt herself drift back in time, back to a Lake Tahoe beach, and a boy named Kade, and a kind of love that lasted forever.

A kind of love she no longer believed in.

Chapter Four

ONCE MEGAN ALLOWED THE MEMORIES, they came like old friends and took her back to a place when she was barely more than a child.

She and her younger brother had lived a life that seemed idyllic to everyone, especially Megan. They had a home with a swimming pool in West Palm Beach, and every summer they took family vacations. After work her father would come in from the garage, drop his keys in the apple jar by the telephone, and clap his hands. "Where's the best kids in the world?" he'd ask.

When she was a little girl, Megan would wait for him by the front window and at the sound of his voice she would run and jump into his arms. Her father wasn't very tall, but to her he was strong and bigger than life. Once when Megan was six years old, her father had been teaching her how to ride a bike at Farlane Park. He jogged alongside her, and when she grazed a tree and began to fall, he caught her by the waist and kept her from hitting the ground.

Caught her in midair.

It was something Megan never forgot. When she was older, her brother did the running and jumping, and Megan would call from the next room, "Hey, Dad, how was your day?"

And every evening he'd find her and kiss the top of her head.

When he was home, that was.

31

Now she knew that her parents had often been fighting, arguing over whether her dad was sleeping with other women or stepping out secretly without her mother knowing it. But Megan and her brother had no idea.

Not until the day their father walked out.

She could still hear her parents' voices, the way they sounded that awful day. Hear them as clearly as if they were standing beside her bed. At first Megan hadn't believed the loud noises could be coming from her parents. She figured her father must've been watching something on television. Her brother was only seven that spring, and he played in his room, unaware that the story of their lives was being rewritten in the kitchen below.

Megan had gone to the top of the stairs and listened. That's when she realized the loud, angry words weren't coming from the TV at all, but from her parents. Her parents, who never yelled at each other. Megan had felt the blood drain from her face. She sat down, hugged her knees to her chest, and concentrated on what they were saying.

"Walk out now, and don't bother coming back!" The words had belonged to her mother, and they terrified Megan. *Walk out? What was that supposed to mean?* Daddy had just come home from work, and they hadn't eaten dinner yet. He would never have gone back out now.

"I didn't want it like this." Her father's voice hadn't been as loud, but it was filled with fury. "You're the one who made the phone call."

"Of course I made the call." Her mother's tone rose a notch. "I find a receipt for roses in your coat pocket? When you haven't given me flowers in five years? The phone call was a natural, Paul. The florist was more than willing to give me your girlfriend's name, so blame him."

"Okay, I've got a girlfriend. What're you gonna do about it?"

"No, Paul, what're *you* going to do?" Her mother sounded half crazy, desperate.

"Nothing." The word was an explosion in the kitchen below. "There's nothing I can do now."

"Yes, you can! You can tell her it's over, tell her we're going to get counseling and try to work things out. Tell her you have a family."

"No, Terri. *You* have a family. I have a job and a mortgage and bills to pay. The kids barely know me."

Megan gripped the staircase and closed her eyes. Her head spun and she felt sick to her stomach. What was her father talking about? Of course they knew him. Whenever he was home they read books together and went for walks and . . .

That's when she'd realized something. Her father hadn't been home much since Christmas, really. Once in a while she'd heard her mother comment about the fact, but never with so much shouting. Megan hadn't thought anything of his absences. Her father was a banker, a busy man, and sometimes his work kept him out late. That was all it was. Right?

Her mother began to weep, a loud, wailing cry Megan had never heard before. "Forget the girl, Paul. I can if you can." She was shrieking, panicking, and the sound of her voice made Megan's heart race. "Don't leave us now, please, Paul. Think about the kids!"

That's when the shouting and crying and angry words had suddenly stopped. Her father's voice was calm once again, and he said only two words, the last words

Megan ever heard him say.

"Good-bye, Terri."

That was it. Nothing about even hearing her mother's plea or possibly breaking up with the girlfriend, whoever she was. No final words of love passed on to the kids, no words of concern for Megan and her brother. Just "Good-bye, Terri."

Megan had held her breath as she peered down into the foyer and watched her father leave. She could still see him, the way he stood by the door with a single suitcase in one hand, a briefcase in the other, dressed in his business clothes. He gave one last look around the living room, then he turned and walked out, shutting the door behind him.

At first Megan had figured it was some kind of bad joke, or maybe even an awful nightmare. A girl in Megan's third-grade class had a father who left them on New Year's Day, and a few years later Sheila Wagner's mother ran off with the assistant principal.

But never, in all her imaginings, had Megan considered such a thing could happen to her family. After all, her family went to church on Sundays and prayed before every dinner and kept a Bible on the coffee table downstairs.

Fathers didn't run out on families like that, did they?

Megan had swallowed her fears, and for the first two days she said nothing about what she'd seen and heard at the top of the stairs that night. But on the third day, her mother pulled her aside and choked out the truth. Her father was gone, and until he came home they'd have to fend for themselves. Her brother was too young to understand what had happened, and their mother told them only that Daddy wouldn't be home for a while.

Looking back, Megan figured her mother held on to

that idea—that her father would come home one day—for the next two months. Then in June, something happened and Megan's mother no longer peered out the window after dark looking for their father's car to pull up in the driveway.

The day school was out, they set off in the station wagon for Lake Tahoe—where Aunt Peggy lived. The only explanation Megan and her brother got was that they all needed some time away.

Four days later they arrived at Aunt Peggy's house on the lake. Her brother was in the pool before they unpacked. That entire first day, Megan did nothing but sit at the far end of the living room and pretend she was reading a book. Really, she was listening to her mom and Aunt Peggy talk about her father. Something about the money he was sending and some kind of papers he'd had delivered to her.

"At least the jerk's sending you support," Aunt Peggy said, and then she shot Megan a glance. "Megan, honey, why don't you go out and play with your brother?"

By that point, Megan had felt sick to her stomach going on two months straight, and when her aunt suggested she leave the house, Megan was more than happy to go. She didn't understand exactly what her aunt and her mother were talking about, but it was something bad, something about her father. And Megan knew deep in her heart that her daddy wasn't coming home, maybe not ever.

She wandered outside, past her brother splashing in the pool, and through a thicket of pine trees out onto the beach. It was a private stretch of sand shared by only the houses in Aunt Peggy's neighborhood. Megan kicked off her shoes and walked along the shore about a hundred yards until she spotted a fallen tree trunk. She sat at one end, stared out at the water, and wondered.

Why had her father left, anyway, and where was love? Was it real? If people like her parents could split up, how could it be? And what about her and her brother? Since he'd been gone, their dad hadn't called or visited. Not once. So what was the point of growing up and getting married if it all fell apart in the end?

If only her father would come home. Then she would know love was real after all, and that God answered prayers.

"Where are you, Daddy?" Her whispered question mixed with the breeze rolling off the south end of the lake and sifted through the tree branches behind her. But she heard no answer.

Tears filled her eyes, and she blinked them back. She'd always done her crying in private, and this wasn't the time for tears. *I miss you.* She gazed up at the sky to a place she wasn't quite sure existed. *I want him to come home and kiss the top of my head like he used to. God, you can make miracles happen, so please make one happen now for me.*

As she sat there a little while longer she realized something. Her father's routine—the way he came home each day and showered Megan and her brother with attention—had been something that made her feel safe and protected. Now, without him, Megan felt unattached, like she was falling without a parachute.

She was about to head back to her aunt's house when something in the opposite direction caught her eye. A boy, about her age, was walking a white Lab along the beach. He noticed her, and before she could escape, the boy waved and headed over.

"Hi." He came up and stood in front of her. "You must be new."

36

Megan shrugged and tried not to feel interested. The boy had clear, blue eyes and something about the way he looked at her made her feel as though he'd known her forever. She struggled to find her voice. "Just visiting."

"Us, too. My grandpa lives here. We come up each June." He sat down a few feet from her on the fallen log. "I'm Kade."

"I'm Maggie."

He hesitated a minute, and a smile played on his lips. "Okay, Maggie, tell me this. If you're on vacation, why're you sitting here looking like it's the end of the world?"

For some reason, Megan felt safe with the boy. She tilted her head and felt the pretense fade from her expression. "Because it is."

Kade's smile dropped off like the bottom of the lake. "Ya wanna talk about it?"

And Megan had.

For the next week, she and Kade met out on the shoreline and talked about everything from the meaning of life to Kade's passion for baseball and his dream of playing in the big leagues. But whenever the topic would turn to Megan's father and her situation, Kade would tell her the same thing: Real love never fails, and where there is that type of love, there is hope. Always.

Kade's father was a minister at a small church in Henderson, Nevada, just outside Las Vegas. His daddy had told him that in a town nicknamed "Sin City" it was important to know what real love was.

"But what about when love dies? Like it did for my parents?" They were walking along the beach, their arms occasionally brushing against each other.

"Maybe they never understood real love." Kade

stopped and picked up a flat rock from the sand. He skipped it across the water and turned to her. "You know, the kind of love in the Bible. The love that Jesus talks about."

That was another thing. Megan had never met anyone her age so versed in Scripture. Not that he talked about it all the time. In fact, they spent most of their hours playing Frisbee or swimming in her aunt's pool or splashing in the lake. One day she found a dozen pale purple azaleas growing wild near a clump of bushes just off the beach.

"Here." She picked the prettiest one and handed it to Kade. "So you'll remember me."

"Okay." The hint of a smile played on his mouth, and his eyes sparkled. "I'll put it in my Bible and save it forever."

They teased and laughed and played hide and seek among the pine trees that lined the beach. But each afternoon as the sun made its way down toward the mountains, she and Kade would find their place on the fallen log and he'd say something profound about love or God's plan for her life. Something that didn't make him seem anything like a fifteen-year-old boy.

Late one afternoon, she narrowed her eyes and studied him for a minute. "You sure you're not an angel or something?"

"Yep, that's me." He let his head roll back, and his laugh filled the air around her. "An angel with a mean fastball and a .350 batting average."

She breathed hard through her nose. "I'm serious, Kade. What kind of kid knows about love like that?"

"I told you." His cheeks were tanned from the week in the sun, and his eyes danced as the laughter eased from his voice. "My dad's a preacher, Maggie. The

Bible's like, well . . ." He gazed out across the water. "It's like the air in our house. It's all around us."

"And the Bible talks about love?"

Megan hadn't known anything about the Bible, really. Sure it sat on the coffee table, and she and her family had gone to church once in a while when they were little. But never in the past few years. Especially not since her father left.

Kade pulled one leg up and looked at her. "The Bible talks all about love. How it's kind and how it never fails."

On their last afternoon together, Megan admitted something to him, something she hadn't really understood until then. "I want to believe, Kade. In love . . . in God . . . in all of it." She let her gaze fall to her hands. "But I don't think I know how anymore."

Kade slid closer to her on the fallen log and took her fingers in his. "Then what you need, Maggie, is a miracle. So that one day everything we've talked about will really happen in your life."

"A miracle?"

"Yep." He scooted closer still and tightened the grip he had on her hand. "Close your eyes, and I'll pray."

Then, while a funny, tingling sort of feeling worked its way down Maggie's spine, she and Kade held hands, and he asked God for a miracle for her, that her father would come home and that no matter what else happened or didn't happen, one day she would know the type of love that never failed.

They made a plan then, that they'd meet there on the fallen log every June, so long as their families came to Lake Tahoe. Before she left, Kade hugged her and gave her the briefest kiss on the cheek. "I'll pray for you, Maggie. Every day. That you'll get your miracle." He gave her a sad smile. "See ya around sometime."

When she and her mother and brother left for home the next day, Megan couldn't decide what to feel. She hated leaving Kade, but her heart soared with a hope she hadn't felt before the trip, and she found herself convinced of several things. First, that God was real, and second, that He was going to give her the miracle they'd prayed for. That one day she'd know for herself a kind of love that didn't walk out the front door one night before dinner. A love that never failed.

Chapter Five

CASEY PULLED OPEN THE BLINDS and stared up between the buildings that surrounded his apartment. Rain, again. Cold, driving rain. He pulled away from the window, padded across the living room, and found his running shoes. Rain was good. Clean and honest and simple, reducing the moment to nothing but Casey and the air he breathed. Besides, the café wouldn't open for another hour and now, while it was still dark, there was nowhere he'd rather be than running the streets of New York City.

Rain, sleet, or snow, he would run.

Three days had passed since his anniversary, and still Casey couldn't pull himself from the past. Crazy, really, that a calendar day could send him into a tailspin of memories and longing. Anniversaries, birthdays, Valentine's Day, Christmas. The trigger was any day the two of them would've been together.

Freedom was out on the pavement, where it always was. Running gave Casey a chance to think about life the way he couldn't at his crowded café or in the confines of an apartment where every square inch held memories of Amy.

He laced up his shoes and noticed that his shoulders felt lighter, as though the mountain of sorrow and regret he lived under couldn't follow him out onto the streets. Three flights down the ancient stairs that ran through the core of the apartment building and he was outside. A wind gust slapped him in the face and sprayed his cheeks with rain. The air was colder than it looked, but it was clean, and Casey sucked in three mouthfuls as he set off.

Five minutes later it happened, the same thing that happened every time he ran. The early-morning commuters and sounds of the waking city faded to nothing, and Casey gained entrance to a world where Amy was still alive and memories of her came easily. A world where he could catch a glimpse of the place where she and their son still lived, where the pain of existence was dimmed—if only for an hour.

He'd run enough over the past two years that come spring he was going to do a marathon. Why not? He would put in the miles one way or another. It gave him a reason to run more, something to tell Billy-G and the regulars at the café. He was training. Not that he needed the time to relive his past or sort through how he could've done something different that awful day, how he could've helped save Amy and the baby.

He had to run to be ready for the race.

Since Saturday, he'd used his running time to indulge himself in the rarest luxury of all. The luxury of going back to the beginning, back to the days when he and Amy first met. Casey brushed his gloved hand over his face and wiped the rain off his brow. He had to be careful how often he did this, this going back to the beginning thing. Because each time he allowed himself, the sound of her voice, the feel of her hand in his were more vivid. Intoxicatingly vivid.

And each time it was harder to find his way back to real life.

But here, on this rainy Tuesday morning, Casey didn't care. One more time wouldn't hurt. Besides, memories were all he had left, all he'd ever have. And they were worthless if he didn't spend time with them every now and then.

He turned right and headed toward Central Park, no longer seeing steamy manholes and cabdrivers vying for early riders. Instead he was in Port-au-Prince, Haiti, his sleeves rolled up and sweat beading on his forehead.

From the time he started high school, Casey had known what he wanted to do in life. He had no intention of becoming a preacher or a doctor or any of the things his parents had figured for him. He would get his MBA and do something different, something where he could keep his own hours and be his own boss, work around all types of people. Then he'd meet a nice girl, get married, and have the kind of life his parents had shared.

But first, he would travel.

A month after he graduated from high school, he turned down three track-and-field scholarships for a one-year position working as a driver for an orphanage in Haiti. The job paid nothing but food and expenses, but it taught him more about life than he could've learned in a dozen college courses.

He drove a twenty-year-old pickup truck with boarded sides and an engine that started only half the time. At first the road conditions terrified him. Traffic ran in multiple directions without any clear sense of right-of-way, and people honked their horns as often as they hit their gas pedals. Vendors littered the roadways, and children darted into traffic at every intersection waving rags and squirt bottles, hoping to make a dime or two by cleaning a dirty car window.

The food was rice and beans and an occasional skimpy chicken leg. Meat wasn't refrigerated in Haiti, showers were scarce, and hot water unheard of. Every mosquito bite carried the threat of malaria. During the day, when Casey was driving the streets of Port-au-Prince, not only was he an oddity because he was American, but he was often the only white person amid hundreds of thousands of teeming people on the main thoroughfare. Casey knew enough Creole to say, "I'm here for the supplies," and "I'll be back next week," and a few other key words, but the language barrier felt like the Great Wall of China. Rats ran the floor of the orphanage at night, and at times the adjustment period felt as if it would stretch on forever.

But after a month in Port-au-Prince, Casey felt more comfortable. He no longer noticed the strange looks he got from people he passed on the streets, and the traffic was somehow invigorating. When he took the time to smile, people treated him kindly. He spent his days getting supplies, shuttling children to various appointments, and helping the ministry team when they staged outreaches on the street corners.

At the end of the first year, Casey signed up for a second.

"What about college?" His father had been worried, but not nearly as much as his mother.

"Have you gone mad?" Her voice was pinched with fear. "Universities won't wait forever."

Casey figured they would. He was still in great shape and ran the hilly side streets at the far end of Port-au-Prince four times a week.

Halfway through his second year, a group of high school youth-group students came to the orphanage for spring break. Casey had been in the driveway on his back, working on the muffler of the old pickup truck, when the students filed through the high security gate.

He paused, taking in the group of them as they made their way into the complex.

That's when he saw her.

She was at the end of the line, listening to one of the counselors point out details about the orphanage, and Casey did a double take. Even looking at her upside down, he could feel his breath catch in his throat. She wasn't striking in the typical sense. Her hair wasn't streaked with blonde, and she wore no makeup. She was a simple kind of beautiful, like wildflowers scattered across an untouched mountain pasture. Casey's hand froze in place, the wrench poised a few inches above his sweaty forehead. She didn't yet know he was alive, and already something in her light brown eyes had worked its way into his heart.

Casey picked up his pace, ignoring the way his legs screamed for relief. The pain of running felt good, especially now. He blinked and allowed the memories to continue.

Her name was Amy Bedford. By that evening Casey had found out enough about her to know that his first impression had been right on. She held no pretense and spoke with a wisdom that was far beyond her sixteen years. The youngest of five girls from central Oregon, her father was a science teacher for a small public high school, her mother a homemaker. Amy's sisters were in college, anxious to get degrees in something other than education and move on to anything more lucrative than a teacher's salary.

Not so Amy.

"My dad's the best man I know," she told Casey that night. "He's touched a thousand hearts in his lifetime, and I want to do the same." She rested her elbows on

45

the old wooden table. "How 'bout you?"

"Well . . ." He gripped the bench he was sitting on and straightened his back. "I want to open a café."

"A café, huh?"

"Yeah." He gave a few thoughtful nods. "I can be my own boss, make my own hours, and meet new people every day." His heart felt light at the prospect. "I've been thinking about it for a while."

"Wow. I never met anyone who wanted to open a café."

Quiet filled the space between them for a moment. "My parents aren't real thrilled about the idea."

She smiled then and said something Casey would remember for the rest of his life. "Someday I want to eat there, okay? At your café."

Casey wasn't sure if it was her faith in his dreams or the sincerity in her voice or the way her skin glistened in the hot, humid night, but with every passing hour he felt himself falling for her. The week passed in a blur of painting the orphanage kitchen and talking late into the night. Three years separated them, but Casey didn't notice a minute of it. Amy was as true as an orphan's smile, guileless and able to speak her mind. Something about her made Casey want to wrap his arms around her and protect her from anything cold or cynical, anything that would dim the warmth in her smile.

They finished the kitchen and moved into the room where twenty-two orphans slept on eleven small wire cots.

"Let's paint the door red," Amy told him.

"Red?" Casey made a face and flicked his paintbrush at her. "Why red?"

"Because." She tapped her brush on the tip of his nose. "Red is the color of giving."

And so they painted the orphans' bedroom door red.

On Amy's last night in Port-au-Prince, Casey asked if he could write to her.

"Yes." They were sitting on a bench in the orphanage courtyard just before midnight and the air around them was stagnant, silent but for the sound of a distant drumbeat. She lowered her chin and locked eyes with him. "I'd like that."

He wanted to kiss her, but he didn't dare. He was on staff, and she was a student, a minor. Instead he swallowed and tried not to notice the way their shoulders brushed against each other. He dropped his voice a notch. "Know something, Amy?"

"What?" She leaned back against the crumbling façade of the orphanage wall and met his eyes again.

"I had fun this week."

"Me, too."

"I'm . . . well, I'm gonna miss you."

She nodded, and her eyes glistened, hinting at tears. "I have to go. The counselors want us in bed by twelve."

"I know." He smiled so she wouldn't see how hard it was to say good-bye. They'd be gone in the morning before sunup, and chances were he'd never see her again. "Be safe."

"And get that café going." Her chin quivered, and she hesitated just long enough to draw another breath. Then she reached into the pocket of her jean shorts and pulled out a folded piece of paper. "Here." She tucked it into his hand. "I've been practicing my Creole."

He started to open it, but she closed his fingers around the paper before he had a chance. "After I go." She took a few steps back and then turned and ran lightly up the steps. When the door closed behind her,

Casey opened the piece of paper and saw that she'd written only three words.

Me reme ou. . . . I love you.

Chapter Six

CASEY HAD ALREADY RUN FOUR MILES—more than his usual route. But today the memories were crisp and vivid. He would've run to California if it meant giving them a reason to continue.

And so he kept running, his strides long and even, eyes straight ahead.

Me reme ou.

He could still see the words, the way she'd scrawled them on that piece of paper. The truth of what she'd written had dropped his heart to his knees and made him certain that somehow, someway, he would see her again. They wrote to each other for the next six months, and by the following summer Casey had enrolled at Oregon State University and made plans to move to Corvallis.

He'd visited the campus just once and met with the track-and-field coaches. Running the hills of Port-au-Prince had paid off, and he was offered a full scholarship. Casey was thrilled, but by then he was convinced of one thing. His future wasn't in running or jumping or throwing a javelin.

It was in business.

And OSU had exactly what he was looking for. An excellent business school and a full-ride scholarship. And something else.

A twenty-minute drive to Amy Bedford's house.

His parents knew nothing about Casey's attraction to

Amy because Casey wasn't sure about it himself. In some ways, even with their letter-writing—the week he'd shared with Amy in Haiti felt like a wonderful dream, as surreal as nearly everything about his time there.

After he enrolled at OSU, he returned home to his parents, sat them down one night after dinner, and broke the news.

"I . . . I thought you'd go to a Christian college, Casey." His mother's lips drew together. "You've been gone so long, and now, well, you'll be gone again."

His father crossed his arms. "Your mother's right, son. You can't learn much about God at a place like OSU."

It was a moment of truth, and Casey gripped his knees. "Dad . . ." He met his father's gaze. "I already know about God." Silence stood between them for a moment. "Maybe it's time I learn something about people."

In the end, his parents agreed. Where better to practice his faith than out in the real world? Despite their reservations, they sent Casey off with their full support.

"Be careful," his mother warned him the night before he left. "The Northwest is a liberal place, and the girls . . . well . . . they don't have the same standards you're used to."

Casey had to stifle a smile. "Okay, Mom."

He had only one girl in mind, and they met up again that September, a couple of hours after his first day of classes, at a coffee shop just off campus. Amy was seventeen by then, a high school senior. The moment she walked through the door of the shop, Casey knew his feelings for her weren't some sort of strange dream.

She moved across the room, past the other tables. Even from ten yards away Casey could see how her eyes danced. When she sat down, he took her hands in his and struggled to find his voice. "There's something I have to tell you, something I couldn't say in a letter."

Curiosity mingled with hesitation and took some of the sparkle from her eyes. "Okay." She studied him. "Tell me."

He waited until he could find his voice. "Me reme ou."

Turning back wasn't an option for either one of them. The next fall, Amy joined him at OSU, and four years later they married and left the Northwest for a small apartment in Manhattan and the chance for Casey to open the café he'd always dreamed about.

"It's perfect, Casey." Her eyes would light up every time they talked about it. "Let's make it happen."

Casey's Corner was still a crazy idea to his parents, but never to Amy. She took a job at a local preschool and stood by Casey as he got the loans he needed to open his shop. On the weekends, they worked side by side decorating and collecting memorabilia for the walls. At the grand opening, no one was prouder than Amy.

The years that followed blurred together like a kind of larger-than-life tapestry of brilliant reds and oranges and thoughtful shades of blue. She had been everything to him—his closest friend, his confidante, his greatest support. Losing her had been like losing his right arm, and the pain of it made every breath an effort.

Even after two years.

Casey slowed his pace to a walk. He had worked his way through five miles of trails—two more than usual—and he was only a few blocks from the café. The

51

memories had been stronger than usual, more vivid, and he fought the urge to keep running.

What was wrong with him anyway? If he could feel like this after two years, maybe he'd never move on, never find a way to get through life without her. Maybe this hazy underwater feeling of going through the motions was how life would always be. His breathing settled back to a normal rate, and he locked his eyes on a narrow stretch of sky as he walked. She was up there somewhere, probably elbowing God in the ribs, bugging Him to give Casey a reason to live again.

His café was a diversion, for sure. He spent most of the week there—talking to customers, helping Billy-G behind the counter, fixing up the place so it never lost the look Amy had given it way back when. But nothing about it made him feel alive, the way Amy had made him feel.

He reached the café and stared at the front door. Someone had hung a fall wreath on it, plastic leaves of orange and red and yellow and a nervous-looking turkey at the center, poking his pinecone head out at everyone who walked by. Thanksgiving was in a month and after that, Christmas.

Amy's favorite time of the year.

Casey gritted his teeth and pushed the door open. He zigzagged his way past a dozen tables, chatting with the regulars and saying hello to a few newcomers. It wasn't until the morning rush was gone that he sauntered over to the counter and dropped onto one of the barstools.

"Hey, Billy-G."

His friend wiped his hands on his apron, reached beneath the counter, and pulled out a section of newspaper. "Saved this for you." Billy-G took a few steps closer and spread the paper out in front of Casey.

"Something you need to think about."

Casey kept his eyes on the old man. "Not another one." He was always telling Casey about a support group here or a Bible study there. "I'm fine, Billy-G, I don't need your help."

"Yeah, okay." The man tapped at the paper. "Everything's great." He began to walk away. "Just read it."

Billy-G was back in the kitchen again when Casey released a long, slow breath and let his eyes fall to the newspaper. It was a small, two-column story, buried deep in the *Times'* Metro Section. The headline read "New Program Pairs Willing Adults with Grieving Children."

Casey blinked and thought about that for a moment.

Grieving children? People were hurting all over the place, people who'd lost sisters or uncles or husbands or friends. But grieving children? It was something Casey hadn't considered.

The article was only five paragraphs, and he gave himself permission to read it. When he finished, he picked it up, held it closer, and read it again. After the third time, the idea began to sink in. It was both simple and profound, really. A children's group in Chelsea had designed a program called Healing Hearts, a way to pair up grieving children with single adults. Children who had suffered the death of one or more parent would be linked with single adults. The article provided a phone number for people to call if they were interested.

Casey imagined for a minute Amy sitting beside him, breathing the same air, sharing his every thought and knowing the things in his soul before they even came into focus.

"It's a perfect idea, Casey," he could almost hear her

saying. "Let's make it happen."

There was a problem, of course.

He wasn't any other single adult; he'd suffered his own loss and maybe the program director would hold that against him, maybe his own grief would minimize his ability to help a hurting child. But he doubted the program organizers would turn him away. Somewhere out there in the big, vast city was a child who needed a mentor, someone to help bridge the gap between his old life and the life he'd been forced to live these past two years. A child who needed love and direction and a reason to live the same way Casey, himself, needed it.

He could make the call and go through the screening, let the organization set him up with a child, and find a way to bring a little light back into both their lives. There were a hundred places where he could take a child in Manhattan, places where the two of them could find an on-ramp back to the highway of the living. Yes, he could make the call, and in maybe only a month or so he could—

"Interesting, huh?"

Billy-G's gruff voice interrupted Casey's thoughts, and he dropped the paper to the counter. "Yeah."

"So?"

Casey folded the paper in half and slid it a few inches from him. "So what?"

"Whadya think?"

"I think you ask too many questions, Billy-G." Casey stood up and gave his friend a half smile. "I also think it's time I get going. I'll be back for a few hours around dinner."

"I knew it." Billy-G's smile held a knowing.

"Knew what?"

"You're gonna call."

Casey shrugged. "I'll think about it."

"Okay." Billy-G gave a few soft chuckles. "You do that."

Casey turned to leave, desperate to appear noncommittal. The idea was too fragile, too new, to expose it to the light of open conversation—even with someone like Billy-G. He needed to play it out in his mind first. Important decisions were always that way for him, taking root and growing in the hidden places of his heart before making their way out into the open.

Casey turned around before he left. "Great job today, Billy-G."

His friend peered at him over his shoulder through the small window that separated the kitchen from the front counter. "Make the call."

"See ya." Casey raised his hand and headed toward the front door.

Under his arm was a folded-up newspaper. And stirring across the barren plains of his heart was something he hadn't felt in a little more than two years.

The early-morning winds of hope.

Chapter Seven

THE BAD GUYS were getting the upper hand. The first part of November was always this way, and Megan was suddenly too busy to worry about real love or long-ago summers or even her own lonely son. Crime was up 11 percent from a month ago, and Megan had two murder-one cases spread across her desk. Months like this could make or break a prosecutor, and Megan wouldn't be broken by anything.

Besides, things were okay at home. Jordan's behavior had improved some, and she was making a point of lying down with him for a few minutes every night before he fell asleep. Maybe that was all her son had needed, after all. A little more one-on-one time.

The idea was as comfortable as a bed of nails.

Who was she kidding? It was like her mother kept saying. Jordan needed a man in his life, someone to wrestle with him and lift him onto his shoulders and take in a basketball game with him every now and then.

"You work too much," her mother had told her the night before. "You'll never find a father for Jordan with your schedule."

The comment had made Megan's cheeks hot, and Jordan's letter to God came to mind as it had nearly every day since she'd read it. "I'm not looking for a father for Jordan. Life doesn't work that way."

"It could, Megan." Her mother's voice was softly persistent. "It could if you'd look for it."

Megan huffed and planted her hands on her hips. "You didn't exactly go looking for a father when I needed one."

Her mother had been silent for a moment, and a handful of emotions flitted across her eyes. Shock and anger, shame and regret. "I was wrong, Megan." She stood and took a step toward her bedroom. "You're young. Don't make my mistakes all over again. It's not fair to Jordan . . . or yourself."

The conversation had played again in Megan's soul several times that day, even as she held conversations with judges and researched precedents for her current cases. *Don't make my mistakes all over again. It's not fair to Jordan . . . or yourself.*

Megan pushed back from her desk and drew in a sharp breath.

It was nearly six o'clock, and she had two more hours of going over briefs and depositions before she could go home. The office was quiet, most people gone except for a few evening clerks and an occasional assistant, finishing up whatever assignment had been passed down from one of the district attorneys.

She stood and headed down the hall to the break room. A cup of coffee would clear the cobwebs, stop her from thinking about her mother's words and her son's sad eyes and the letter he'd written to God. It wasn't her fault things were such a mess. She and George hadn't exactly been given a choice about how their lives had played out.

The break room was empty. Megan went to the coffeemaker, grabbed a tall Styrofoam cup, and poured herself some coffee. She opened the freezer door on the refrigerator, took two ice cubes, and dropped them into her cup. She liked her coffee black and lukewarm. Hot coffee took too much time to drink.

She was holding her cup, stirring the ice cubes with her little finger, when her eyes caught something on a folded section of the *New York Times*. Someone had placed the paper beneath the coffeemaker, and it had collected a circle of brown spots around the base of the pot. A headline showed near the top, and without meaning to, Megan read it.

"New Program Pairs Willing Adults with Grieving Children."

She stopped stirring and set down her cup. A program for grieving children?

The newspaper was stuck to the bottom of the coffeemaker, and Megan lifted the pot, careful not to tear the article. She slid it out and held it close as she read through it. A children's club in the city had set up a program called Healing Hearts that would pair adults with children who had experienced the death of one or both parents.

Suddenly Megan didn't need the coffee. Her hands were shaking as though she'd already had five cups. A program for grieving children? It was exactly what Jordan needed! Megan left her cup on the breakroom counter and took the newspaper back to her desk. The club was probably closed at this hour, but it was worth a try.

She picked up the phone and punched in the numbers. Someone answered on the first ring.

"Manhattan Children's Organization, may I help you?"

Megan opened her mouth, but no words came. Tears filled her eyes, and with her free hand she massaged the lump in her throat until she could speak. "I . . . I read about your program."

The woman on the other end identified herself as Mrs. Eccles. "We have quite a few programs, ma'am. Could you be more specific?"

"Yes . . ." Megan found the newspaper once more, and her eyes darted over the text. "It's the Healing Hearts program. My . . . my son is a child like that."

"I see." The woman's tone was noticeably softer. "Well, then, the first step is for you and your son to come down and fill out the paperwork, give us a chance to meet you and interview both of you. Then we'll try to pair your son up with one of our male volunteers as quickly as possible."

"You have . . . volunteers waiting for children?" The idea knocked the wind from Megan. Why hadn't she heard of this sooner? She glanced at the date on the newspaper and saw that the article was nearly two weeks old.

"Yes, ma'am. The program's quite popular." She paused, and Megan heard a rustling sound in the background. "Can I sign you and your son up for an appointment?"

Megan thought of all she had to do at work, the depositions and briefs and precedents that had to be studied. An appointment would take time, maybe an entire afternoon. Time she certainly didn't have. A single teardrop rolled down her cheek, and she dabbed at it with the sleeve of her silk jacket. "Yes." She sniffed quietly and closed her eyes to stave off any more. "Yes, I'd like that very much."

The appointment took place a week later, and four days after that Megan took the call at work. It was Mrs. Eccles, and her voice rang across the phone line like a kind of early Christmas carol. "I have good news for

you, Ms. Wright. We've found a match for your son."
Megan leaned back in her office chair and held the
phone more tightly to her ear. "You have?"

"Yes. I think you'll be quite happy with our choice."

"Is he . . . is he young or old?" Megan's voice was
breathy, and she could see the buttons on her blouse
trembling with every heartbeat. Jordan hadn't stopped
talking about the program since they signed up. "Tell
me about him, please. Did he . . . has he always wanted
to help children?"

"Well . . ." The woman hesitated. "His story's a bit
different than most."

Megan's shoulders fell a bit. Wasn't that the point of
the program, pairing children with adults who had a
strong desire to help a lonely boy or girl?
"Then . . . why did you pick him?"

"His wife died a few years ago, delivering their first
child. The baby didn't make it, either." Some of the
cheerfulness faded from the woman's voice. "He saw
the article about Healing Hearts and was very interested.
Thought maybe it'd be good for both him and a hurting
child."

Remorse tapped at the door of Megan's conscience.
"Oh." She wanted to let excitement grow within her
again, but it all seemed so sad. "I'm sorry." How could
a man with that type of loss be any kind of positive
influence on Jordan? She kicked her doubts back into
the closet and pinched the bridge of her nose. "What
else? Tell me about him."

The woman gave as thorough an overview as
possible. The man's name was Casey Cummins. He was
thirty-four and ran his own café in Midtown. He was
interested in basketball, football, baseball, and anything
outdoors, and, because of his job, his hours were

flexible.

"He jogs three miles a day and has a master's in business administration. He'd be happy to help with homework."

Megan glanced at the murder files on her desk and felt the door to her closet of doubts creak back open. "What about the screening process?"

"We went over that at the interview."

Megan crossed her arms and pressed her fist into the hollow near her lower rib cage. "I know that, but tell me anyway. I'm a district attorney, remember?" She paused and forced a more polite tone. "Specifically . . . how did this Casey check out?"

"No record of any criminal behavior with either the FBI or the local police. He's never served time, never been arrested, no history of drug abuse. Never even had a speeding ticket, as far as we can see. He pays his bills on time and has an apartment about twenty blocks from his café. We spent several hours interviewing him here at the office, and of course we had a licensed social worker check out his residence."

"And . . ." Megan hated her suspicions, but after a week of waiting, the whole setup sounded too good to be true.

"We give our volunteers a rating, Ms. Wright. It's not something we usually share with the child's parent, but in this case—given your job—I think it might be okay to tell you. Mr. Cummins earned the highest possible marks in all categories. He's the kind of volunteer we're desperate for."

Megan exhaled and felt herself relax. "So, then. When do they meet?"

"Today's Monday. . . . The woman's voice drifted off, and Megan heard her flipping pages. "Fridays are good for him, so let's try for this Friday, November 14, say three o'clock?"

She shot a look at her own calendar. A hearing would take up most of the afternoon, and normally Megan would use early Friday evening to go over her notes from the past week. Still, maybe there was a way to make it work. "I have to be there, right?"

"Yes." Megan could feel the woman's disapproval. "Of course. You'll come in with Jordan, and the two of you will spend an hour or so getting to know his special friend. Then, if you're all comfortable with the idea, Mr. Cummins can spend another hour or so with your son either at the club or across the street at the park."

"Right." Megan pictured Jordan, the way his eyes would light up when he heard the news. He deserved this; she believed that with all her heart. Work would simply have to wait. "Okay, that'll be fine." She killed a heavy sigh before it could escape. "Three o'clock Friday."

As she hung up, Megan realized something. Already she was looking forward to Friday, to meeting this Casey man and watching the way he might interact with her son. It was a wonderful idea, one that didn't rely on her dating and coaxing someone into being a surrogate father for Jordan. Healing Hearts was a program based on honesty and need, where expectations and guidelines were spelled out from the beginning.

Jordan and Casey would get together once or twice a week and possibly speak on the phone. All of them would meet with the counselors at the Children's Organization every month to discuss how the relationship was progressing, and to give each of them a chance to ask questions or air concerns.

Of course it was a good thing, and it was worth every

minute of work she might have to forfeit to see that the setup was successful. Megan had planned to wait until after work to tell Jordan about the phone call, but suddenly she couldn't think of anything else. She picked up the receiver again and dialed her home number. Jordan answered after only a few seconds.

"Hello?"

His young voice filled her heart, and her eyes felt watery. "Hi, honey. It's Mom."

"Hi! When're you coming home?"

"Soon." She gazed out her window and tried to picture his face. "Jordan, I got a call from the Children's Organization today. You know . . . the ones trying to find you a special friend?"

Jordan sucked in a loud breath, and his words were louder and faster than before. "You mean . . . they found him?"

"Yes . . . yes, they found him." A sound that was part laugh, part sob slipped from Megan's throat, and for a few seconds she covered her mouth with her fingertips. "In fact, I think they found someone just right for you, buddy."

The phone was ringing as Casey slipped through his apartment door and tossed his jacket on the chair. Work had been busy, but the wind gusts were worse than usual. At least once for each of the last ten blocks he'd thought about giving up and grabbing a taxi. But he'd pressed on, and now he was glad. He felt alive and awake, the same way he'd felt since doing the interview with the people at the Children's Organization.

He hadn't even been assigned a child yet, and already Healing Hearts was living up to its name.

He darted around the back of his old, worn sofa into

the kitchen, and picked up the phone just as the answering machine clicked on. "Hello?" He cradled the receiver between his cheekbone and shoulder and tore the gloves from his hands. The moment his fingers were free, he punched the Off button on the answering machine. "Hello?"

"Yes, hi, this is Mrs. Eccles at the Manhattan Children's Organization. We've matched you up with an eight-year-old boy, and we were wondering if you were available to meet him this Friday?"

The room began to spin. Casey felt behind him for one of the kitchen chairs. He positioned it and sank to the seat. "This Friday?" His words were little more than a whisper, and he repeated them again. "This Friday, the fourteenth?"

"Yes." The woman gave a happy laugh. "If that works for you."

Mrs. Eccles had said it could take six weeks to make a match between volunteers and children, but Billy-G had disagreed. "Two weeks tops." He had given a wave of his favorite spatula. "I have a feelin'. Two weeks, Casey."

Indeed.

Casey switched the receiver to the other hand and leaned back in the chair. "Friday would be perfect. Tell me . . . tell me about the boy."

"Okay." Mrs. Eccles drew a quick breath. "Well, he's a darling little guy, eight years old and midway through second grade. He likes a lot of the things you like, and he lives with his mother and grandmother on the Upper East Side."

"His father?" Casey almost hated to ask because the answer was obvious. The boy wouldn't be in the program if his father were alive.

"The man was in his fifties, a bond trader who died of a massive heart attack a few years ago at work. Since then the boy's mother and teachers have noticed a change in his behavior, enough that he's had counseling and other help. He's responded lately to spending more time with his mother." Mrs. Eccles hesitated. "Unfortunately, his mother is a district attorney, and she can't be home with the boy as often as she'd like."

The picture was as clear as air. The boy's mother loved him enough to sign him up for the program. But on her own, she simply couldn't make up for all the boy had lost when his father died. Casey stood and poured a glass of water. He wasn't dizzy anymore, but a certain kind of giddiness had come over him.

A child needed him!

He was about to get involved in the life of an eight-year-old boy, something he was certain Amy would've wanted him to do.

Mrs. Eccles was going over some of the details, and Casey tried to focus on what she was saying. Something about coming at three o'clock and expecting an hour-long meeting with the boy's mother, and possibly having another few hours with the boy after that. Then, if the first meeting went well, he'd be given the boy's phone number and address.

"If Friday's a success, you can take the boy out for pizza. Something to break the ice."

Casey wrote "pizza" across the top of a pad of paper.

The woman was about to hang up when Casey remembered something. "You didn't tell me his name."

"Oh . . . sorry." He could hear a smile in the woman's voice. "His name's Jordan."

It was all Casey could do to finish the phone call. The boy's name was Jordan? How was that possible? He hung up the phone and walked across his apartment to the bedroom he'd shared with Amy. Her journal still lay in the nightstand beside their bed, and now he opened the drawer and pulled it out.

The book was worn and flimsy, with a light tan leather binding. Amy had saved favorite sermon notes and Bible verses on pieces of paper that still stuck out every twenty pages or so. Casey held it carefully, as though any sudden movement might break it in half. Inside the front cover, Amy's name was barely visible, scrawled in blue ink across the center of the page.

It was the same journal she'd had with her in Haiti, the year Casey had first met her.

He ran his fingers across the letters of her name and flipped past the accounts of how the two of them had met and the detailed feelings she'd had for him even back then, past the entries she'd made when they were dating, past every other passage, all of which she'd shared with him many times.

Then, at the back of the journal, he found it.

A list of baby names, names Amy and he had discussed and agreed on for their first child. He already knew what he'd find on the list, but he had to look anyway, and as his eyes scanned the names he saw he'd been right.

Amy had thought she was having a boy, but they'd come up with names for both a boy and a girl—just in case. The list held ten names, five for a girl, and five for a boy. And next to the name they liked best, Amy had doodled a happy face.

Her favorites were written over several times and stood out in bold on the finely pressed piece of paper. Kaley for a girl, and for a boy they'd chosen the name they'd most easily agreed upon.

Jordan Matthew.

Casey stared at the name and imagined the odds that Mrs. Eccles would pair him up with a boy named Jordan. Seconds passed, and chill bumps rose on Casey's arms and across the back of his neck. What was it Amy liked to say? Something about Christmas miracles. Yes, that was it. She used to tell him that Christmas miracles happened to those who believed.

He would tease her and tell her she was wrong. With her in his life, miracles happened every day of the year. But she had been adamant, insisting that something special happened to people at Christmastime, and that Christmas miracles were there if only people looked for them.

Casey shifted his gaze to the picture of Amy that hung on the wall nearby. *Were you right? All this time . . . ?*

If Christmas miracles really were a special kind of something that happened once a year for those who believed, then Casey was certain that wherever Amy was at that very moment, she was smiling down at him, glowing with that special something that had won him over so easily the first day he met her.

Because here and now, six weeks before Christmas, Casey was suddenly convinced that a miracle was in the works, and that somehow it involved an eight-year-old boy named Jordan.

Even if the two of them wouldn't meet until that Friday afternoon.

Chapter Eight

GOD HAD FINALLY READ HIS LETTER.

That was the only way Jordan could explain the things that were happening to him. He and his mother had spent more time together the past month than all the months before as far back as Jordan could remember. And then she'd found out about the special program. Healy Hearts. At least that's what Jordan thought it was called, not that it mattered, really.

The important thing was, God had found him a daddy.

Well, not a daddy really, but a pretend daddy. Someone who would play with him every week and take him to the park and help him with his pluses and minuses the way Keith's daddy helped him.

Jordan was so excited about the whole thing, he could barely sleep. He'd lie in bed and stare at the blue-and-white-striped wallpaper and the little row of baseball gloves and bats that went around the top of his room, and picture God getting his letter and opening it and knowing that the program, the Healy Hearts thing, would be the perfect way to give him a daddy.

He tried not to, but lots of times that week he asked his grandma questions about that coming Friday.

On Wednesday he found her and tugged on her sleeve. "How many days, Grandma?"

"Until what?"

"Until I meet him. How many days?"

His grandma let out another huffy breath and patted his head. "Two days, Jordan. One less than yesterday. Don't keep asking."

"Do you think he'll be nice?"

"Very nice."

"Should I tell him my knock-knock joke about the chicken and the bulldog?"

"Sure, Jordan, tell him the joke." His grandma turned her attention back to the television. "Most men like jokes."

"What if he wants to be my daddy, Grandma. What then?"

"Jordan . . ." His grandma put her hands over her face and sort of stretched out the skin on her forehead until the bunches disappeared. "Your mother already talked to you about that. The man's name is Casey, and he won't be your daddy. Just a special friend."

"But kind of like a pretend daddy, right, Grandma?"

"No, Jordan. Not like a pretend daddy. Like a special friend. That's what he is, a special friend."

"Oh." Jordan thought about that for a minute. "But if he wants to move in with us, can he sleep in my bedroom?"

Grandma took tight hold of the arms of her chair and her eyes got wide. "He won't be moving in with us, Jordan. You need to understand that. Not now and not ever."

"Okay." Jordan waited until his grandma turned back to the TV one more time. Then as soft as he could, he did one more tug on her sleeve.

"My goodness, child." Grandma's voice was louder than before, and her eyebrows disappeared into her forehead. "Can't you leave an old woman in peace?"

"Just one more question." Jordan made his voice nice

and quiet, the way Grandma liked it. Then he smiled just in case she might say no.

"Oh, bother." Grandma slid down a little in her big chair, and her bones got smaller in her shoulders. "Go ahead."

"What if . . . what if he doesn't like me?"

Grandma sat up straight again, and her eyes got softer. "Of course he'll like you." She reached out one arm and gave him a half hug. "Just don't ask him a hundred questions."

By Friday morning, Jordan was so excited he couldn't eat breakfast. This time the questions went to his mother. How many hours until they could meet him? What would he look like? Where would they go and what would they do? And most of all, what if Casey didn't like him? His mommy was starting to breathe hard, and Jordan was sure she was going to get mad at him, when all of a sudden she did something really strange, something she never did when she was getting ready in the morning.

She laughed.

Then she messed up his hair and set a glass of orange juice down in front of him. "Jordan, I don't have all the answers this time. Besides, I should be the one asking how many hours until we meet him." She planted her hands on her hips. "Because then you'll finally have all the answers you need."

Jordan laughed, too, but after that he tried not to ask any more questions the rest of the morning. His mother was right. She didn't know all the answers, but God did. And a little while later, on the way to school, Jordan added a P.S. to his letter. A P.S. was when you wrote a letter and remembered one more special thing you forgot to say.

His mother was reading one of her files, so Jordan looked out the window of the cab and made his P.S. extra quiet. So only God could hear.

"P.S., God. Please make Casey like me."

Jordan hardly listened to Miss Hanson that day, and twice he had to sit at the back of the room for not paying attention. But that didn't matter because when the bell rang, his mother picked him up in a taxi, and off they went to the kids' club, the place where he was going to meet his pretend daddy.

Except he wasn't going to tell that to anyone else, just himself. Because other people would call Casey a special friend, and that was his 'ficial title. But Jordan knew the truth. They walked in, and the same lady they met before took them to a room, and just then his mommy's pager went off.

"Phone call," she said. She smiled at the lady and held up her finger. "Just a minute."

When his mommy hung up, she talked to the lady in private for a long time, and Jordan heard only a few of their words. Something about an emergency situation and how it would never happen again and that his mother was very sorry. Then the lady from the club gave Mommy a mean sort of look and did a frowny face for a long time and said just this once maybe.

Finally, Mommy and the lady came over to him.

"Sweetheart"—his mother scrunched down so they were the same size—"Mommy has a special meeting at work, and I can't stay to meet Casey. Not this time." She looked at the other lady. "But Mrs. Eccles will stay with you after Casey comes, and everything will be fine. I'll meet him next week, okay?"

Jordan had a hurt feeling in his heart, but he decided this wouldn't be a good time to cry. Besides, his

71

mommy had special meetings all the time, and at least he was still going to meet Casey. "Okay."

His mom left, and after another minute, Mrs. Eccles came back, and this time she had a man with her. A man who looked tall and strong and happy like Brett Favre of the Green Bay Packers. He walked up and held out his hand and did a kind of smile that made Jordan feel all warm and safe inside. "Hi, Jordan. I'm Casey."

"Hi, Casey." Jordan shook the man's hand, and right then and there he knew for sure. Casey was a pretend daddy, not a special friend. Because sometimes Jordan dreamed about having a daddy again, and every time the daddy in his dream looked the same way.

Tall and strong and happy, and exactly like the man standing in front of him right now.

Casey had to wait five minutes before he could meet Jordan, all the while listening to Mrs. Eccles rail on about Jordan's mother leaving early.

"I mean, it's the first meeting!" The woman gave several short shakes of her head. "No one leaves early at the first meeting."

Casey didn't really care. He hadn't given much thought to Jordan's mother. It had been meeting the boy that had kept him up at night and put an extra spring in his step as he jogged to work and back each day that week. New York City was the prettiest place in the world at Christmastime, and already the transformation was taking place. The first snow had fallen, and Central Park was white except the paths and play areas. Police were making provisions for the Macy's Thanksgiving Day Parade, and lights were being wound into trees and along storefronts throughout Manhattan.

The closer Friday drew, the more Casey thought that

Amy must've been right after all. Christmas miracles did happen to those who believed, and somehow, some kind of miracle was definitely coming together for him and Jordan.

Mrs. Eccles finished explaining that this time—against her better judgment—she was going to let Casey meet Jordan even though the boy's mother wasn't there, and finally Casey was ushered into the room where the child was waiting. The moment he saw the boy, he had the strangest sense. As though somehow he'd seen the child before, maybe at the café or at the park somewhere.

He took the boy's hand in his own and shook it, and in that instant Casey felt it. A bond, a connection so quick and immediate he could compare it to only one thing—the way he'd felt when he first met Amy.

They spent an hour talking with Mrs. Eccles, and by the time Jordan started telling knock-knock jokes, Casey and the social worker nodded at each other and knew it was time.

"Hey, Jordan, wanna go play at the park?"

The boy's eyes lit up like the tree in Rockefeller Center. He shot a look at Mrs. Eccles. "Can we?"

"Yes. Your mother said it was okay."

They set off, and Casey held Jordan's hand when they crossed the street. The feel of the child's small fingers protected inside his own did strange things to Casey's heart. Was this how it would've felt to hold the hand of his own son, his own Jordan, if the boy had survived?

Casey took the boy to the East Meadow play area, the one with the big slide where he and Amy had come so many times before. As they rounded the corner, Jordan spotted the play equipment and did a series of excited jumps.

"Hey, Casey, guess what? This is where my mom takes me to play sometimes."

"Really?"

"Really!" He pulled Casey toward the tall slide. "Only she doesn't go down the slide with me, but that's okay 'cause she's a girl."

Casey laughed. "I'll go." He followed Jordan up the ladder. "But don't make fun of me if I get stuck, okay?"

Jordan giggled, and the two of them went down the slide one after the other until Casey lost track of how many times. The bench Amy and he had shared was only a few feet away, but Casey refused to look at it. Finally, after half an hour, he sucked in a deep breath and pointed toward the swings. "How 'bout I push?"

"Would ya?" Jordan's eyes grew wide, his cheeks ruddy from the cold wind and excitement. "My mom doesn't do that a lot, either. Pushing can break the heels on her shoes."

"I'm sure." Casey stifled a laugh. After a few minutes of pushing Jordan he tried to picture the boy's mother, how hard it must be to have a demanding job and a son as lonely for attention as Jordan clearly was. "Tell me about your mom."

Jordan stretched out his legs and made the swing go a few feet higher. "What about her?"

"Well, like, does she go to parties or out on dates or stuff like that?"

"Nope." Jordan leaned back and stared at the sky as the swing moved him up and down. "She only works."

"Oh." Casey wasn't sure what else to ask. He didn't want to upset the boy on their first time out. "She must like her job."

"She's a district attorney. Megan Wright." Jordan looked over his shoulder at Casey. "She's in the newspapers a lot."

Casey let the woman's name swing from the rafters of his mind for a moment. It sounded familiar, in a distant sort of way, and then he remembered. One of the regulars at Casey's Corner had a son who'd been shot and killed in a robbery a year ago. Megan Wright was the prosecutor, Casey was almost sure. Yes, that was it. The boy's father had said Megan Wright was tough as nails, one of the reasons Manhattan was still a good place.

Casey gave the boy another push. "I think I've heard of her."

"Yeah." Jordan's tone was less than excited.

"So that's why she works so much, huh? Because she has so many cases?"

Jordan shrugged and dragged his feet along the sandy gravel beneath the swing. When he came to a stop, he turned to Casey and narrowed his eyes. His expression made him look years older. "She doesn't believe in love."

Casey's heart slipped several notches. He stuffed his hands in the pockets of his jeans and gave a few slow nods of his head. "Is that right?"

"Yeah." Jordan kicked at the gravel and looked across the play equipment to a couple walking hand in hand beside two small children. "She told Grandma that my daddy didn't know how to love her and now . . ." He raised his small shoulders again. "Now that Daddy's gone, she doesn't believe in love anymore."

"Oh." Casey felt a shudder pass over him. "That's too bad." What must the woman's life have been like for her to feel that way? To have lost all faith in love? His customer had figured out the woman perfectly. Tough as nails. Both in the courtroom and out, if Jordan's

75

assessment was true. He pictured her, locking away criminals as deftly as she locked away her feelings.

No wonder Jordan needed a special friend.

"What time is it?" Jordan rose off the swing and cocked his head. He'd given Casey a glimpse of his heart, and Casey was grateful for it.

"Time to get going."

The two of them started back, and for a while they said nothing. Casey looked at his watch. "We have enough time for pizza, if you want."

Jordan's face lit up, and he did a few more quick jumps. "Pizza's my favorite. Extra cheese and pineapple, but not with those slimy black things, okay?"

"Olives?" Casey chuckled and took the boy's hand. "Okay, we'll skip those."

"Yeah, olives." Jordan pinched his face up in a knot. "Yuck! They look like chopped-up eyeballs."

Casey laughed again, and he was struck by something. He hadn't had this much fun since before Amy died. The two of them crossed the park and found a small pizza place Casey hadn't visited before. He ordered and they took a booth near an old, broken jukebox. Eventually, he'd take him to Casey's Corner but not yet. It was too soon in their friendship to have people asking questions and introducing themselves.

Midway through a large extra-cheese pizza with pineapple, Casey leveled his gaze at Jordan and lowered his voice.

"I've been thinking about your mom."

"Yeah, I wish she coulda come. She said she'd meet you next week."

"Good." Casey caught his red plastic straw between his fingers, drew it close, and took a long swig of ice water. "But I meant something else."

Jordan looked up from his pizza, curious. "What?"

"Okay, here it is." Casey gave a slow look over first one of his shoulders, then the other, as though the information he was about to share with Jordan were top secret. "My wife used to say that Christmas miracles happen to those who believe."

"Christmas miracles?" Jordan's eyes got wide.

"Yes." Casey stroked his chin. "So, maybe this is a good chance to see if my wife was right. You know, if Christmas miracles really *do* happen."

Jordan tilted his head and set his slice of pizza down on his plate. "Do you think they happen?"

"Well—" Casey hesitated. "I didn't used to." He took his straw and downed another mouthful of water. His eyes never left Jordan's. "But now something tells me they're true, that Christmas miracles really do happen."

"Hey, I know what you mean! I wrote a letter to . . ." Jordan's eyes lit up, but then his expression changed. He paused and changed his words. "What I mean is, I believe in Christmas miracles . . . if you do, Casey."

"Then that's what your mom needs. A very special Christmas miracle."

Jordan's chin dropped slowly to his chest. "I don't think she believes in miracles. Not any kind."

"Well, then . . ." Casey sat up straighter, the mock conspiracy over. He wanted to know about the boy's letter and a hundred other things, but those questions could come later. Ten or twelve pizzas into their friendship. "If she doesn't believe, then that's what you and I can pray for."

Jordan's eyes got wide. "That Mommy will believe in miracles?"

"How 'bout one thing at a time." Casey bit his lip. "Let's pray that she'll believe in love again. That's always a good thing to pray."

"Yeah . . ." Jordan gave him a lopsided smile. "Then if she believes in love, maybe one day she'll believe in miracles, too, right?"

"Right." Casey wanted to say that by the sounds of it, if Megan Wright believed in love again, she would have to, by default, believe in miracles. Because it would take one to accomplish the other. But instead he nodded to the pizza. "Let's wrap up the rest for your mom. We have to be back in ten minutes."

"Okay." Jordan bit off a mouthful of pizza and washed it down with a swig of root beer. "Thanks for taking me out, Casey. I had fun."

"Me, too." A strange feeling wrapped itself around Casey's heart, and he gave a little cough to clear his throat. "I think we'll be special friends for a long time."

An hour later when Casey was back at home, he did something he hadn't done in months. He went to the edge of his bed, dropped to his knees, and thanked God for bringing Jordan Wright into his life. And for the alive feeling that still stayed with him, coloring his thoughts and soul and everything about the coming days. When he was done thanking God, he bowed his head and prayed for something with an intensity he hadn't known since his days in Haiti.

That Megan Wright would believe in love again.

When he was finished, he changed clothes, brushed his teeth, and after an hour of watching ESPN, slipped into bed earlier than usual. He pictured Amy and tried to imagine what she would've thought of Jordan. She would've loved him, of course. And if she knew anything about the boy's mother, Casey was sure that somehow he and Jordan weren't the only ones praying for Ms. Wright.

Somewhere up in heaven, Amy was praying, too.

Jordan told his mommy about the pizza and the park and the swings and the twenty-three times they slid down the big slide together. He talked the whole way home and through dinner and even after he brushed his teeth and Mommy tucked him into bed.

That's when she put her finger against his lips. "Enough, Jordan. It's bedtime."

Jordan took a long breath. "He's the best special friend in the world, Mommy. Wait till you meet him and then the three of us can—"

"Jordan . . ." She smiled and kissed him on the tip of his nose. "I'm sure he's wonderful. It makes me happy to see you so excited, but right now you need to get to sleep. We can talk about it more tomorrow."

He watched her leave the room, and after she closed the door he sat straight up in bed and looked out the window next to his bookshelf. "God, it's me. Jordan." He smiled real big. "Casey's so cool, God. He's the best. I'm so glad You sent him for me." A little bit of the smile slipped off his mouth. "Casey says we need to pray for Mommy, that she'll believe in love again." Jordan tucked his legs up beneath him so he could see the stars better. "That's why I'm here, God. And if You want, I'll write You another letter. Because if You can send me someone like Casey, I know You can make this happen. Especially at Christmas.

"Because Casey says that's when You make the bestest miracles of all."

Chapter Nine

MEGAN HAD HEARD CASEY'S NAME so often in the past three weeks, he seemed like part of the family.

She splashed water on her face and dried her cheeks with a hand towel as the voices wafted in from the dining room.

"Then he took me to Chelsea Piers, Grandma, and we rode the roller coaster and that spinning ride, and after that we ate a big pile of blue cotton candy, and he played pinball with me for five straight games even after I beated him, and . . ."

It was Saturday morning, and the previous night had been Jordan's third with his special friend. No doubt the Healing Hearts program had been the perfect solution for Jordan, and Megan had been able to give more of her attention to work because of it. Her son was happier, more at ease, and doing better at obeying his grandmother after school. Besides, when was the last time she'd taken him to Chelsea Piers?

Jordan's special friend had even taken to calling a few times a week, chatting with her son and asking about his day at school. The man seemed every bit the perfect volunteer Mrs. Eccles had made him out to be.

But sometimes a fingernail of doubt scratched the surface of Megan's conscience.

The program held no guarantees, really. No binding contract that could keep a single man like this Casey from walking out of her son's life and breaking his heart. Megan studied her reflection in the mirror for a moment and liked what she saw. Without her makeup she looked younger than her thirty-two years, and with Jordan happy again, the tiny lines at the corner of her eyes had faded.

She shut off the light and headed to the dining room.

"There you are." Her mother tossed her a pointed look. "Your eggs are getting cold."

Saturday mornings Megan's mother made breakfast, and Megan used the opportunity to sleep a little later than usual. She smiled at Jordan. "Sounds like you had another fun Friday."

"Yeah, but how come you had to cancel again?"

"I told you." Megan took the chair between Jordan and her mother and unfolded her napkin across her lap. "Fridays are busy for me, Jordan. It's hard to get away."

"That's what you said last week." Jordan didn't sound rude, just disappointed. "Casey really wants to meet you."

Megan angled her head as she balanced a forkful of eggs. "Does *he* say that, or just you?"

"Well . . ." Jordan thought about that for a minute. "He doesn't actually say that, but he thinks it. I know he does, Mom. The lady at the club says all the other parents have met their child's special friend except you."

Megan made a mental note to contact Mrs. Eccles and ask her to keep her comments to herself. Her frustrations should not be vented at Jordan.

Next to her, Megan's mother finished a piece of toast and dabbed her lips with the corner of her napkin. Her voice was more pleasant than before. "So, dear, exactly how old is this Casey? Is he a college boy?"

Jordan's voice rose a notch, his face filled with enthusiasm. "He's thirty-four, and he owns his own restaurant." Jordan looked at Megan and then back at his grandmother. "Isn't that cool?"

"Very cool." Her mother's tone took on a new level of interest. She made a subtle look in Megan's direction. "Thirty-four, single, and owns his own restaurant." She paused and the corners of her smile lifted a bit. "Sounds like you should make time for the meeting, Megan."

"Mother . . ." Megan leveled her gaze at the older woman and lowered her voice. "I'm not interested. And I hate when you push."

"Mommy?" Jordan sounded forlorn. He tapped her hand with the end of his fork until she looked at him. "You don't wanna meet Casey?"

Megan raised her eyebrows at her mother and then made a quick shift back to Jordan. "Of course I want to meet him, honey. Next Friday for sure, okay? I'll clear my schedule."

"Good, then I'll call Casey today and tell him."

"Tell him what?"

"That he should get three tickets for the Nets game, not just two."

"Hmmm." Megan's mother stood up with her empty plate and walked to the kitchen. Her voice still had that cheerful matchmaker tone Megan hated. "Sounds like a date to me."

"Wait a minute!" Jordan jumped up from the table and ran to the drawer near the telephone. "That lady from the kids' club gave me a letter for you. She said it was extra important that you read it." He grabbed an envelope from the drawer and jogged back to Megan. "Here." He hesitated. "Read it, Mom. What's it say?"

Megan slid a single sheet from the envelope, opened

it, and read silently to herself. It was from Mrs. Eccles, and it was short and to the point.

Dear Ms. Wright: We have tried on several occasions to contact you and relay to you the importance of your presence at a meeting with your son and his special friend. Parental involvement in the program is absolutely essential. Because you missed three consecutive meetings here at the club, we are giving you the opportunity to set up a meeting with Jordan and Mr. Cummins outside the arranged Friday meeting time. Below you will find the man's home and cell-phone numbers so that the two of you can find a way to meet. If you do not follow through with this program stipulation, we will be forced to remove Jordan from the program and assign Mr. Cummins to another child. Sincerely, Mrs. Eccles.

"Well, Mommy, well . . ." Jordan gripped the edge of the table and did two little jumps. "What does it say?"

Megan stared at her son, not sure what to tell him. Her mother was in the kitchen washing the frying pan and mercifully wasn't there to add her own questions. The nerve of the social worker, threatening to remove Jordan from the program. So what if she hadn't met this . . . this Casey, whoever he was. He was Jordan's special friend, not hers. Why were the people at the Children's Organization so set on the fact that parents be involved?

Her questions dissolved like springtime snow.

It didn't matter if Megan agreed with the rules, she had no choice but to play by them. Jordan had lost one man in his life; she wouldn't stand by and watch him lose Casey, too. Not because she hadn't done her part to follow the program guidelines.

"Jordan . . ." She folded the letter and slipped it back in the envelope. If they had to meet, they might as well get it over with. "How would you like to have Casey over for dinner?"

"Yes!" Jordan ran in a tight circle and made his trademark jump straight into the air, his fist raised toward the ceiling. "That'd be the best thing in the world, Mom! When can he come?"

Megan thought for a minute. She could get her Sunday work done early and share a meal with the man tomorrow. That way, she could call Mrs. Eccles on Monday and tell her the requirement had been met. Besides, her mother had bridge on Sunday nights, so no one would be around to pressure Megan into anything more than a casual dinner meeting. She smiled at Jordan. "How about tomorrow?"

"Yes! Yes . . . yes . . . yes . . ." Jordan darted over to the phone, grabbed the receiver, and ran it back to Megan. "Here!" He was out of breath, his eyes vibrant and alive. "Here, Mommy. Call him now."

From the kitchen her mother had caught on to what was happening, and she had the knowing look of a Cheshire cat as she dried the frying pan. Megan clenched her teeth and managed a smile. "Your friend doesn't know me, honey. Why don't you call. Tell him six o'clock, okay?"

Jordan raised his shoulders a few times and grinned. "Okay. I'll call his cell phone." He punched in numbers that had become familiar to him over the past few weeks, and the following conversation was short. When Jordan hung up he smiled big at Megan.

"He was at work. He says he'll be here at six." Jordan set down the phone, wrapped his arms around Megan's legs, and squeezed. "Thanks, Mom. I just know you'll love him as much as I do."

Megan couldn't figure out why she was nervous.

It was a few minutes before six on Sunday evening. She'd made meat loaf and baked potatoes and everything was ready, but still she had a funny feeling. What if they clashed somehow? What if he'd read about her work in the paper and didn't like female prosecutors? What if the evening ahead of them made Casey care less for Jordan than before?

Megan banished her thoughts and turned off the oven just as the doorbell rang. She ran her fingers through her hair one last time and watched as Jordan tore out of his room and raced for the front door.

"Casey!" He opened it and shouted the man's name at the same time. "Come on, I'll show you my room!"

"Hold on a minute, buddy. I think I'd better meet your mom first." The door opened a bit more, and a man appeared in the entryway, holding hands with Jordan. He was tall and broad-shouldered, and he wore faded jeans and an NYC sweatshirt. His dark hair was cut close to his head, and his eyes were a kind of clear blue, like the water off the Florida Keys. And something else, something familiar Megan couldn't quite figure out.

She set a pair of pot holders down on the counter and joined them in the living room. "I'm Megan. Thanks for coming."

"Casey." He nodded once and shook her hand. "Thanks for having me."

An awkward silence planted itself between them, but only for a few seconds. After that, Jordan tugged at Casey's arm again. "Come on, I have to show you the transformer plane you gave me. It's all set up and

85

everything!"

Casey and Megan chuckled and exchanged a quick smile. "I better take a look."

"Go ahead. We'll eat in a few minutes."

Megan had dinner on the table in no time, and with Jordan filling in every spare moment, there was no need for conversation between the two of them. Finally, Megan had to tell him to stop talking and eat. The moment Jordan was quiet, Casey turned to her, his expression polite and guarded.

"Jordan tells me you take him to the East Meadow, my favorite play area. The one with the big slide."

"Yes, we've always—" Megan stopped herself. "Wait . . . that's where I've seen you."

Casey set down his fork and cocked his head, confused. "I don't remember meeting."

"We didn't meet." Megan could see the moment clearly in her head now. "You jog, don't you?"

"Every day."

"A month ago I took Jordan out to play, and I think that was you sitting on a bench at the back of the play area by yourself." Megan could suddenly see the pain in the man's eyes that day, and she chose her words carefully. "Jogging suit, knit beanie. You seemed kind of pensive."

Casey looked from Megan to Jordan. "Okay, now it's coming together. This whole time Jordan was familiar to me, like I'd seen him somewhere before." He hesitated and shifted his attention back to Megan. "That was a long day for me, the day I stopped on the bench. At work, I mean. I saw Jordan playing, and I thought he looked like . . . like a nice boy."

Megan searched Casey's eyes and saw holes in his story big enough to drive a truck through. But they were none of her business. Besides, the dinner meeting was only a formality. She forced a polite smile. "Small world, then."

"Very small."

Jordan jumped back into the conversation, and they talked about the past baseball season and whether the Nets would have a good run this year or not.

Casey turned away from Jordan for a moment and caught her eye. "Jordan told me to get three tickets for Friday. Will you join us?"

Megan was trapped. She lowered her fork to her plate and looked from Jordan to Casey. The man was only being polite, but Jordan was practically desperate for her to say yes. "Sure." A sigh stuck in her throat, and she swallowed it. "I'd love to go."

"Cool! We'll have the best time!" Jordan ate a bite of potatoes and looked at Casey again. "I got flash cards in my room for pluses and minuses. If you wanna do 'em after dinner."

"Sure, buddy, I love flash cards."

The easy conversation continued, and Megan did her best to stay out of it. That way she could watch this man, the man she'd seen at the East Meadow play area that day, and wonder about his past. He'd lost his wife and baby, she knew that much. And certainly that explained the look in his eyes that day at the park. But how had he and her son gotten so attached, so quickly— almost as though they'd known each other for years?

They finished dinner, and Megan cut off the flash card session at seven-thirty. "School tomorrow, Jordan. Sorry . . ."

She and Jordan walked Casey to the door, but Jordan turned around and ran back toward his room. "Don't go yet. I forgot something."

When Jordan was gone, Megan caught Casey's gaze and held it. Now that she'd met him and seen how wonderful he was with her son, she felt awful about not showing up the past three Fridays. "Casey, listen." She kept her voice low so Jordan wouldn't hear her. "I'm sorry about the other meetings. I should've made it a priority."

"No big deal. Tonight'll satisfy old Mrs. Eccles." Casey winked at Jordan as he raced up to them once more and thrust a drawing into Casey's hands. "Besides, we had a good time anyway, didn't we, sport?"

"Yep." Jordan gave Casey a high five and pointed to the drawing. "That's a picture I made for you."

"Wow." Casey admired it for a long moment. "It's perfect. I'll save it forever, okay?"

"Okay." Jordan's eyes danced a little more than usual. "Should we tell Mommy about the prayer?"

"No." Casey gave Megan an easy grin. "Let's make the prayer a secret for now."

"A secret prayer, huh?" Megan gave Jordan a teasing look. "I take it that's a good thing."

"Yes." Jordan gave a hard nod in Casey's direction. "Very good."

They agreed on where to meet for the basketball game that coming Friday and said their good-byes. When Casey was gone, Megan helped Jordan to bed and went to her office to work.

It was only then that she realized she'd forgotten to ask Jordan about the secret prayer. Whatever it was, no harm could come from the two of them praying for her. Even if it had been a lifetime since she'd put any faith in praying. She opened the notes she'd been working on and positioned her hands on the keyboard.

But nothing would come. Not then or any time in the

88

next hour.

At half past nine that evening, she finally gave up trying to work and headed for bed. The last thought on her mind before she fell asleep wasn't about how to win the case on her desk, or expose a witness, or find a missing bit of evidence. It wasn't even about Jordan.

Rather, it was the dimpled smile of a man she'd only just met. A man she felt as though she'd known her entire life, all because of a chance encounter in Central Park.

Casey stayed up late that night, thinking about Amy.

She and Megan Wright had nothing in common. Where Amy was simple, Megan was cultured. Amy's lack of guile was in utter contrast to Megan's cunning in the courtroom. No question Jordan's mother was beautiful, but a woman with a walled-up heart was not someone Casey wanted to spend a lot of time with.

Still, he prayed for her that night, as he had every night since he and Jordan made the deal. A secret prayer, he'd called it earlier that evening. And it was. Because Casey guessed if Megan had any idea they were praying for her to believe in love again, she'd order the whole thing off and forbid it. She had that kind of commanding presence.

Casey was glad Megan had figured out where they'd known each other from. The park, of course. It made perfect sense. If they both frequented the East Meadow, they were bound to have run into each other that afternoon. But as Casey fell asleep in his recliner watching *SportsCenter* that night, he was baffled by a strange thought.

He must've seen the woman only briefly that day at the park. The moment she'd described with him on the bench wasn't one he could remember, because he'd been too caught up in his past to notice a strange woman staring at him from across the way.

But if he couldn't remember seeing her, then why in the world was she so familiar?

Chapter Ten

MEGAN WANTED TO KNOW MORE about Casey Cummins, and she used the Nets game as her chance to find out.

It was halftime, and the two of them were anchored outside the men's room waiting for Jordan. "Casey . . ." She leaned against the wall and nudged him with her elbow. "I have a question for you."

"Shoot."

"Why was it such a long day?"

Casey couldn't have looked more confused if she'd asked him to fly down the stadium stairs. "What do you mean?"

"That day at the park, when I first saw you." Her tone wasn't flirtatious or pushy, just matter-of-fact. She hoped it would make him drop his defenses a little and talk to her. If her son was going to be crazy about the man, she wanted to know more than his name and job description. "Why was it a long day?"

The muscles in his face relaxed some, and the pain Megan had seen that afternoon at the park flashed once more in Casey's eyes. "It was my anniversary. Eight years."

"Oh." Megan let her gaze fall to the tiled floor. "I shouldn't have asked."

"It's okay." Casey slipped his hands into the pockets of his jacket and rested his shoulders against the same wall. "The reason I noticed Jordan was because he made me think of my little boy."

Megan wanted to crawl into a hole. Whatever Casey had shared with his wife, it had been far richer, far more meaningful than the marriage between George and her. She was about to apologize when he spoke up.

"Now it's your turn."

She gave him a sad smile. "That's fair."

He tilted his head back a bit, his eyes locked on hers. "Why don't you believe in love?"

Before Megan's heart had a chance to find a normal rhythm, Jordan skipped out of the rest room and found his place between them. "Mom, can we get a hot dog before the second half? Please?"

In the space above his head, she whispered, "Not now, okay?"

"Okay." Casey grinned, and his expression told her that he doubted she would have given him an answer anyway.

At the end of the night, Casey told them he had a couple of extra tickets to a football game that Sunday at Giants Stadium. This time when Casey asked her to come, Megan found herself agreeing more quickly.

When Sunday arrived, the game was a nail-biter, and by the end of the evening the three of them were yelling at the top of their lungs.

"Nothing like Giants football!" Casey shouted the words above the roar of the crowd.

"Nothing like it!"

By the end of the weekend, Megan felt even more strongly that she'd known Casey Cummins all her life. She kept waiting for his attention to die off, fade into nothing as she expected it to. They'd met the program requirement, after all. Casey's interest was in Jordan, not her. But a few nights later Casey called, and Megan answered the phone. "Hello?"

"Guess what?"

"What?" Megan had kept their friendship very simple and businesslike, despite her probing questions at the basketball game. But at times like this, she couldn't help but feel a little thrill at the sound of his voice.

"It's snowing!" Casey sounded not much older than Jordan.

"Yes." She giggled. "And it's seven o'clock."

"That's the perfect time for skating at the park." He hesitated. "Wollman Rink, Megan. What do you say? You and Jordan get ready, and we'll surprise him, okay?"

"Well . . ." The whole thing made her wonder what was happening to her resolve, her steely determination. But she didn't dare voice her feelings. She'd kept them from her mother so far, and if she had any sense, she'd keep them from herself. After all, the man wasn't looking for a relationship. He was still in love with his dead wife. Besides, nothing smart could come from letting herself fall for Jordan's special friend. She was too busy, her heart too closed, for a man like Casey.

She glanced at the clock on the microwave. "Right now?"

"Ah, come on, Megan. You only live once."

"I don't know . . ." Megan hesitated just long enough for him to pounce.

"Good! I'll pick you both up in twenty minutes."

Jordan was thrilled with the surprise, and he didn't stop talking until, halfway around the rink the first time, Megan fell smack on her backside.

Jordan's face twisted in concern, but Casey stifled a laugh as he held out his hand and helped her up. "If the judges could see you now."

93

"Stop." Megan made a sound that was more laugh than moan. When she did, Jordan relaxed and joined in. She winced as she made her way to her feet and brushed the ice off her woolen slacks. But she didn't fall again the rest of the night, and at the end of the evening Jordan gave Casey a quick hug and ran into the apartment, leaving Casey and Megan at the door still breathless from the adventure.

Their eyes met and held for a moment, and Megan thought of a dozen things she wanted to ask him. What were they doing and where was it leading? And most of all, didn't it feel wonderful to laugh again? But she was certain questions like that would send Casey running. Besides, she was feeling this way only because skating at Central Park in December was somehow magical. And magic didn't always make sense.

The moment passed, and the days began to blend together. Every time she joined Casey and Jordan for an evening out or a few hours at the park, she figured it was the last time, that she was still out of place in their midst because now that she'd fulfilled the program requirement and met Casey, the arrangement was intended for the two of them.

Not the three of them.

But Casey kept inviting her, and she kept hearing herself say yes.

They saw a Christmas play at an off-Broadway theater, and a few nights later he took them to his café. It was warm and brightly decorated with Broadway posters and street signs. A big man behind the counter welcomed Megan and Jordan with a hearty handshake. "So, you're the reason old Casey hasn't been around much, huh?" His smile lit the room.

When Casey sat Megan and Jordan at one of the

tables by the window, she watched him head through the café and make brief conversation with a few of the customers. He was obviously a successful businessman, liked by all types of people. She watched as he made his way back to the counter, and she saw the man behind the counter lean close and whisper something.

Casey only smiled in response and lifted his hands in the air. When he returned to the table, Megan asked him about it. "Okay, what's the story? You're in trouble with your staff because of us, right?"

"Hardly." Casey grinned. "Now, what're we having for dinner?"

As busy as November had been for Megan, December saw the court calendar grind to a halt. Most of the hearings were used only to gain continuations until after the holidays, and Megan found herself looking forward to the time she spent away from the office.

Still, she worried about what would happen come January, when the calendar got busy again and the newness of her friendship with Casey wore off. She had to keep reminding herself that he wasn't in their lives for her, but for Jordan. And she promised herself that after December, she'd let the two of them get back to meeting without her.

"He's falling for you, Megan." Her mother confronted her one day as she was heading off to work. "And you?"

"Don't be ridiculous, Mother. We're grown adults, and neither of us is falling anywhere. I'm only helping Jordan get to know him better."

"Yes, and I'm the Easter Bunny." Her mother clucked her tongue and narrowed her eyes in silence for a long while. "Don't you hurt that boy, Megan. I know you."

"Mother, my goodness. I'm the one who took Jordan down and signed him up for the program. The last thing I'd do is find a way to hurt him where Casey's concerned."

Her mother only lowered her chin and gave Megan a look that shot arrows at her soul. "I'm not talking about Jordan." She paused and dropped her voice. "If you're not falling for him, then don't lead him on."

Anger and frustration mingled and boiled near the surface of her heart. How could she tell her mother that yes, she was falling. Especially when she was almost convinced Casey didn't share her feelings? Besides, she didn't believe in love. Wasn't that her? Maybe her mother was right. Maybe it was time she reminded herself of that fact so neither of them got hurt.

She sniffed hard. "I'm not leading him on. He's a friend, Mother. Nothing more."

The days melted away, and still the three of them continued to find ways to be together. They walked through Central Park and had a snowball fight on the meadow between the tennis courts and the reservoir, and Casey's fingers nearly got frostbitten.

"Where's your gloves?" Megan dropped beside Casey on the closest park bench and watched Jordan as he pelted bushes with one snowball after another.

"Lost 'em at the café last week." Casey shrugged. "I'll live. I can always use my coat pockets."

They shopped at Macy's and saw the lights of the city from a horse-drawn carriage. After her mother's warning, Megan was careful never to so much as let her arm brush against Casey's so that he wouldn't get the wrong impression. And as wonderful as their evenings together were, he never gave her any hint that he was interested in her.

Two days before Christmas, Casey called and talked to Jordan for a few minutes. Then he asked to speak to her.

"Hello?"

"Hey . . . listen, I want to bring by a gift for Jordan. Would tomorrow be okay?"

Megan's heart ached at the sound of his voice. The month was almost over, and she had the strangest feeling that these were their last days together, that after the New Year everything would change. But for now she couldn't bear to miss an opportunity for the three of them to be together again. "That'd be perfect. Why don't you come for dinner? Mom and I make turkey on Christmas Eve."

"You don't mind?"

"Of course not." Megan kept her voice casual. "We'd love to see you."

Jordan was ecstatic about the idea, and Megan's mother promised to be on her best behavior. Casey arrived with a box of roasted almonds and a bouquet of white roses for Megan.

He handed them to her and rubbed his bare hands together. "I hope they're not frozen."

Megan took the flowers and for just the flash of a moment wondered if he'd chosen white over red on purpose. "They're beautiful, Casey. Thank you."

"I figured a New York City prosecutor probably didn't get flowers too often." He looked down at Jordan and handed him a wrapped box. "Besides, your son here wasn't much help with Christmas suggestions for his mom."

"Can I open it?" Jordan held his fingers poised near the crease in the wrapping paper, waiting for the go-ahead signal.

Megan and Casey laughed, and Casey nodded. "Sure, buddy."

Jordan tore off the paper, and inside was the kind of baseball glove he'd wanted for three months. "Wow . . . I can't believe it. Can we try it out; huh, can we?"

"Tell you what . . ." Casey dropped down to Jordan's level. He took the glove and folded it in half near the base of the thumb. "Keep it like this and tuck it beneath your mattress. By the time the snow melts, you'll be able to catch 'em better than McGwire."

The night passed in a pleasant blur of getting the meal ready and eating together. Afterward, Jordan gave Casey a framed photo of the two of them for his café wall, and Megan gave him a pair of gloves.

Red gloves.

"Jordan told me you said red was the color of giving." She tilted her head. "I figured there's no one more giving than you these past few months." Her tone changed and became more teasing. "Besides, without gloves you aren't worth much in a snowball fight."

A sad, distant sort of look worked its way across his expression but only for a moment. "Yep." Then he smiled and slipped the gloves on his hands. "Red's the color of giving, and with these"—he shot a look at Jordan—"I'll be giving some pretty mean snowballs."

When they finished with the gifts, they played Monopoly and watched *It's a Wonderful Life*. Long before the angel got his wings, Megan's mother excused herself for bed and Jordan fell asleep. When the movie ended the TV went dark, and the room was lit only by the glow from the nearby Christmas tree.

Megan was about to carry Jordan to his room, when Casey stood and held out his hands. "Let me."

She sat back down and watched him sweep her sleeping son into his arms and carry him toward the bedroom. *Don't do this to yourself, Megan. Nothing good can come from what you're feeling. It's a shadow, a trick, a hoax. Keep the walls in place, and no one'll get hurt.*

But when Casey walked back into the room, the sight of him made her heart skip a beat. She could hardly order herself to keep the walls standing when Casey's kindness had long since knocked them to the ground.

He poured two mugs of coffee and returned to the spot next to her on the sofa. "Here."

"Thanks." Her voice was softer than before, and she was glad for the shadowy light, glad he couldn't see the heat in her cheeks. "Jordan was tuckered out."

Casey chuckled and shook his head. "I've never known a kid so full of life."

Megan wanted to say that Jordan hadn't always been that way, but she felt suddenly shy, unable to think of the right words. With Casey so close she could smell his cologne, she couldn't decide whether to bid him good night or find a way to stretch the night for another hour.

"Okay." Casey took a swallow of coffee and lowered the mug to his knee. "You can't run from the question this time."

"What question?"

Casey hesitated, and his eyes found hers. She could feel his gentle heart, his concern, and the fact that he wasn't joking. "Why don't you believe in love?"

Megan took a moment to catch her breath. Then she did her best to give him a teasing look. "Why do you want to know?"

"Because . . ." Casey reached out and brushed a section of hair back from Megan's face. The touch of his fingers against her forehead made her ache for his kiss in a way that shocked her. He let his hand fall back to his lap, and his voice was barely more than a whisper. "Because sometimes I think you wouldn't recognize love if it sat next to you at a Giants game."

Megan tried not to read anything into his sentence. Instead she drew a long, slow breath and set her cup down on an end table. "You really want to know?"

Casey nodded. "Really."

"Okay, I'll tell you." Then with careful words sometimes soaked in sorrow, she did just that. She told him about her father and how he'd left their family without warning, and about meeting George and believing their lives together would be everything her parents' lives were not.

"But he didn't love me, either. Not really." She felt her lip quiver, and she bit it to keep from crying. "He wanted me to work, but a few days after I passed the bar exam, I found out I was pregnant."

"He loved Jordan." It was a statement, as though Casey knew more than Megan realized.

"Yes, he did. But it was different with me. I was never more than a business partner to George."

"And that's why? Why you don't believe in love?" Casey's voice was gentle, tender, and something about it made Megan want to tell this man everything, even the things she'd never told anyone before.

"I did believe once, a long time ago." She drew her legs up and angled herself so she could see Casey better. "I was thirteen, and my mother took us to Lake Tahoe, to a private part of the lake where my aunt owned a house." Megan rested her cheek against the sofa cushion. "The first day there I met this boy." She felt herself drift back again, the way she had a few months ago when she'd given herself permission to remember that time in her life.

"Lake Tahoe?" Casey leaned a little closer and sat up. He seemed more alert now, taking in every word Megan said.

"Yes." Megan smiled and felt a layer of tears fill her eyes. "The boy's name was Kade, and that's all I remember, really. Kade from Lake Tahoe. He was fifteen, and he told me something I'll never forget." Megan wiped at a single tear. "He told me real love was kind and good and came from the Bible. A sort of love that never ends." Megan gave a quiet sniff. "He told me he'd pray for me every day, that I'd get a miracle and wind up knowing that kind of love." She reached for her glass again and took a sip. "I never saw him after that. I guess I figured maybe he was an angel."

"Hmm." Casey stirred across from her, and Megan noticed that he didn't look as comfortable as before. What had she said to change his mood? Had the talk about love scared him? Or was he merely missing his wife on another Christmas Eve without her?

"Sorry . . ." Megan looked at her watch and gave a stiff little laugh. "I've bored you and now it's late."

"No . . . no, you didn't bore me, Megan." He slid to the edge of the sofa and moved closer so that their knees were touching. Then he lifted his hand to her face and framed it with his fingertips. "I think it's a beautiful story and one that . . . that doesn't have to have a tragic ending."

It took all Megan's effort to concentrate on finding an answer. The nearness of Casey made her emotions war within her in a way she couldn't sort out. "It . . . it already did. George died before we ever figured out a way to love like that."

101

Casey lifted Megan's chin so that their eyes met and held. "What was your name back then? Your maiden name?"

The question pulled her from the moment and made her want to laugh. "Why?"

"Because . . ." Casey searched her eyes, looking to the depths of her soul. "I want to picture everything about the way you were, back when you still wanted to believe in love."

"Howard was my maiden name." Megan lifted her shoulders. "And I wasn't Megan, I was Maggie. Maggie Howard."

Even in the dim glow of the Christmas tree, Casey's face seemed to grow a few shades paler. Again, Megan wasn't sure what she'd said, but the magic of the moment was gone. Casey stood and gathered his red gloves and the photo of him and Jordan. "I guess I better go."

"Yes." Megan chided herself for being so transparent. A man like Casey had his own ghosts to deal with on Christmas Eve.

They walked to the door, and before Casey left he cupped his hand along the side of her face once more, leaned close, and for a single instant brought his lips to hers. The kiss was over before Megan realized what had happened, and Casey whispered, "Merry Christmas, Megan."

Not until he was gone did Megan realize something. The glistening look in Casey's eyes hadn't been a reflection from the Christmas tree.

It had been tears.

Chapter Eleven

IT WAS A MIRACLE.

No other explanation existed, except that in His everlasting mercy, God had stepped into Casey Cummins's world and handed him a Christmas miracle. The kind Amy had always believed in.

But not the one he'd been praying for these past few weeks. And not one he was sure he wanted. Not yet, anyway.

Casey's head spun, and his heart wasn't sure whether to take wing or drop to his shoes. Under the circumstances he couldn't possibly ride a taxi home, so when he reached the ground level of Megan's apartment he began to walk. Strong and hard and fast into the chilly night, and after less than a block he felt his eyes well up.

He hadn't asked for any of this. He'd wanted only to befriend a young boy, to bring hope and light and healing to a heart that had grieved as much these past two years as Casey's had. If he'd known he would find love, he wouldn't have made the call. Amy deserved more than that. It had only been two years, after all. Two years. How dare he give his heart to someone else after so little time?

His feet pummeled the ground, carrying him south and taking him into Central Park. The lights were still lit, and couples strolled the paved walkways. Casey stayed on the less traveled paths and let the tears come.

He walked until he reached the bench at the back of the East Meadow play area, the place where he and Amy had come so many times before. Then he sat down and dropped the gifts from Megan and Jordan on the cold wood beside him. How was it possible? The whole time while he'd been taking Megan and her son out, God had been orchestrating the events to lead up to this one night, that one conversation with Megan.

And that was something else. What had he been thinking, kissing her?

Amy . . . Amy, if you can hear me, I'm sorry, honey. I love you, still. I'll always love you.

His tears came harder now, and he covered his face with his hands. The thing of it was, it had already happened. All of it. And there was nothing he could do about it. Being angry at God wouldn't change the truth. He loved Megan with a fierceness that scared him, loved her in a way he hadn't even realized until a few hours ago. Loved Jordan, too. And now . . . after what he'd just learned . . . he was certain he would share his life with them, love them and live with them forever.

As sure as Christmas, it was all about to play out.

Casey wished for just a moment that Amy could be there beside him again, to hold his hand and hug him, tell him it was all okay. That none of them could do a single thing about time or the way it marched on without respecting loss or feelings or memories.

That sometimes life could hurt as much as death.

His fingers were wet from his tears, and an occasional icy gust of wind burned against them. He sniffed and remembered the gift Megan had given him. The red gloves. He pulled them from their wrapping once more and slid them onto his fingers. Then . . . as he stared at his hands, he realized something.

Amy had told him that red was the color of giving. That had come from her, not him. And if there was one thing she would've wanted to give him this Christmas, it was the gift of freedom. Freedom from the pain of losing her, freedom from holding on.

Freedom to love again.

She'd given him so much in life, and now, in death, she would give him this. But if that was true, if he was going to let go and move on with life, he needed this time to tell her good-bye. He lifted his eyes to heaven and spoke in a voice that even he could barely hear. "Amy . . . I never wanted it this way, you know that. But . . . it happened. And the way it happened . . . well, it can't be anything but a miracle."

He dried his tears with the red gloves and thought back to the night with Megan. "I love her, Amy. I love her son. Even before I found out about the miracle. And I was wrong about the two of you. I think you would've liked her. Maybe a lot." He felt another tear spill onto his cheeks, and his voice grew tight. "I'll always hold you close inside, Amy. But for now . . . for now I have to let go."

For a long while he sat there, longing for a chance to see her again. Instead he closed his eyes and felt it. Something had released in his heart, and at the same instant, he felt as new and alive inside as the fresh fallen snow. He dried his eyes one last time and stood. Then, without looking back, he jogged to the closest street and hailed a cab.

The time for tears had passed, and Casey grasped the reality at hand. It was December 24, and a miracle no less amazing than Christmas itself was about to occur. Carrying Jordan's gift under his arm, he raced up the stairs to his apartment and headed for his bedroom. The box was at the bottom of his closet near the back corner, tucked behind his clothes in a place where it had been all but forgotten.

Casey slid it out and tore through it until he found the old Bible.

The one he'd had as a fifteen-year-old boy.

Then, as carefully and quickly as he could, he thumbed his way to the back, to the thirteenth chapter of 1 Corinthians, to a place where he was convinced he'd find it. And sure enough, there it was. The pressed purple flower, the one Maggie had given him that week. And written in his own youthful handwriting was this simple sentence:

Pray for a miracle for Maggie Howard.

Casey stared at it until the words faded and became pine trees, tall and proud, anchored in the sandy shore of Lake Tahoe. He'd gone there every summer with his parents, even after he met Maggie. Every year until he graduated from high school he'd looked for her, but she never returned to the lake.

She had seemed so sad back then, so sure that love was a fraud. And he, a preacher's boy, had been so sure otherwise. Love was good and kind and pure and true. Love never failed. Wasn't that the message of his boyhood days, the message his father preached from the pulpit every Sunday?

His name was Kade Cummins, and back then he'd gone by Kade.

But sometime during his freshman year on the baseball team, the players began calling him by his initials, K. C. And in time, it was the only name he knew. Casey Cummins. He'd kept his promise to Maggie, praying for her every time he opened his Bible until he left for Haiti. That year his father gave him a new Bible as a going-away present, and his old one was packed away in a box of baseball trophies and old high school mementos.

He still thought about Maggie often that first year in Port-au-Prince.

But after he met Amy, his thoughts took a different direction, and not until tonight, when Megan told the story, did the pieces all finally and completely fall together. He'd spent years praying for Maggie Howard, praying that she'd find real love one day. And then—when his life had been little more than a chance to remember the past—God had brought the two of them together so that he, he himself, could be the answer he'd prayed for all those years ago.

And it had all happened on Christmas Eve.

If that wasn't a Christmas miracle, Casey wasn't sure what was.

Of course, it wasn't a complete miracle, not yet. Not until he could look into Maggie's eyes, the eyes he'd first met as a boy, and know without a doubt that she believed in love again. The kind of love he'd taught her to believe in back on the sandy shores of Lake Tahoe.

It was nearly midnight, but Casey didn't care. He picked up the phone, punched in Megan's number, and waited. She answered on the third ring.

"Hello?"

"Megan, it's me, Casey. I'm sorry to call so late."

"No . . . no, it's fine. I was up." She hesitated. "Are you okay? You sound like something's wrong."

"Everything's just fine, actually, but I have a favor to ask you."

"Anything, Casey." He could hear the relief in her voice. "Whatever you want."

Casey kept his words as slow and calm as possible.

"Have your mother watch Jordan tomorrow morning at ten o'clock. Meet me at the East Meadow, at the bench near the big slide." He stopped himself from saying anything more. "Please, Megan."

She paused. "Of course. I'll be there at ten."

After they hung up, Casey found a blank Christmas card and began to write. When he was finished, he searched his top dresser drawer until he found an old velvet box. His heart raced as he checked the contents. It might not be a perfect fit, but it would work for what he wanted to do.

Sleep came slowly, in fits and starts, but Casey didn't mind. He couldn't stop thinking about what had happened, and more than that, how the timing was so utterly fitting. Everything was coming together on the most beautiful day of the year, the day when miracles truly did happen all around them.

Christmas Day.

Chapter Twelve

MEGAN ARRIVED at ten o'clock exactly.

It was cold and windy, a Christmas morning when nearly everyone else was still opening gifts and enjoying the warmth of their families. Megan looked beyond the empty play area to the bench at the back near the big slide, the one nestled against the bushes. She pulled her long wool coat tight around her neck, and lifted the collar to ward off a gust coming off the reservoir.

Casey was nowhere.

She checked her watch and saw that it was a minute after ten. Strange . . . Casey wasn't usually late. Careful on the icy gravel, she slowly made her way toward the bench. She was ten feet away when she saw it.

Sitting squarely on the middle of it was a wrapped gift. Megan's heart beat faster, and again she glanced around, looking for Casey. Had he already come and left her this present? It seemed an odd thing to do. After all, he'd brought her roses the night before, and if he'd had another gift, he would've given it to her then.

She shivered and walked the remaining distance to the bench. The gift was large, about the size of a big book. On the top was a card with her name written across the front, and tucked beneath the ribbon was a small pressed azalea, pale purple and tinged brown around the edges of the petals. Megan brought it to her face and breathed in the faint musty smell. Something about the flower was strangely familiar. Where had she seen it before?

She lowered the gift and turned enough to scan the play area. "Casey?" She waited, but there was no response. He must've left the gift, but why? Why here, and why hadn't he waited for her?

She opened the card, pulled it from the envelope, and began to read.

I've prayed for you a thousand times, Maggie Howard. Open your present and turn to 1 Corinthians, chapter 13. Then you'll know what I mean.

Megan's hands began to shake, and once more she glanced around, looking for Casey. A wind gust played with her hair, and she brushed it away from her eyes. Whatever did he mean, he'd prayed for her a thousand times? And why had he referred to her by her maiden name, the name she'd used as a little girl? She took the delicate pressed flower and set it in the card, then slipped them both into her pocket.

Without waiting another moment, she slid her fingers into the seam in the paper, and pulled it off the gift. Beneath the wrapping was an old, worn Bible, cracked and faded from the years. And embossed at the lower right corner was the owner's name.

Kade Cummins.

Megan gasped and nearly dropped the Bible. With her free hand she brought her fingers to her mouth and stared at the cover as everything around her began to tilt. How had Casey gotten Kade's Bible? And what about the flower? Was that the one she'd picked twenty years ago, the one she'd asked Kade to hold on to so he wouldn't forget her? And what did Casey mean by having her open it here, now?

She tucked the Bible beneath her arm and checked the

card once more. 1 Corinthians, chapter 13. Megan slid the card into the front part of the big book, and after a few frantic moments she found the place. There, written in fading ink, were words that made her heart stop.

Pray for a miracle for Maggie Howard.

Nothing made sense, and Megan wondered if she might faint. If this was Kade's Bible, then how had Casey gotten it? And why had he said in the card the prayers had come from him, and not Kade? She was about to gather the Bible to her chest and sit down on the bench when she heard something behind her. Her heart jolted into an unfamiliar beat and she turned around.

"Merry Christmas, Maggie." Casey was coming toward her, his eyes sparkling as he made his way.

"Casey . . . what . . . how'd you get this?"

He stopped a few inches from her, lifted the Bible from her arms, and set it on the bench. Then he took her hands in his and spoke words that made the blood drain from her face. "Kade, Maggie. My name's Kade."

"No . . ." she shook her head. "That's . . . that's impossible. Kade was . . . he was blonde and skinny and freckled and . . . you're Casey . . . you couldn't be . . ." Her voice faded, and she could no longer find the words. As strong as Megan Wright could be in court, she was suddenly thirteen again, desperate to believe in a love that wouldn't fail.

"Maggie, it's me. I promise." Casey must've known she was about to fall. He pulled her closer, let her lean on him for support. "I lost the blonde hair and freckles when I turned twenty. And everyone's called me by my initials since high school."

An explosion of feelings went off in Megan's heart. Disbelief and shock and the overwhelming sense that she was dreaming. "You . . . filled . out." She remembered to breathe.

"Yes." A low chuckle sounded in his chest and he stroked her hair.

"I can't . . . is . . . is it true? You're really him?"

"I am. And see, Maggie, I was right all those years ago, wasn't I?"

She was still too shocked to answer, too amazed that she was in the arms of a man who so long ago had given her a reason to hope, a reason to believe in love. And now . . . now he'd done that all over again before she'd even known it was him.

"Remember the secret prayer Jordan and I had for you?"

"Yes . . . yes, I remember." Strength was returning to Megan's knees, and now her shock was being replaced by an explosive joy and a hundred questions. "What did you pray?"

"We prayed for a Christmas miracle, that you'd believe in love again."

"You did?"

"Uh-huh. Not so different from the way I prayed for you every day back when I was a boy."

Megan peered into his soul. "Kade Cummins, is that really you?"

He didn't answer her with words. Instead, he took her face in his hands and kissed her. Not the momentary kiss from the night before, but a kiss that silenced her doubts and her questions as well. When he drew back, he whispered her name against her cheek. The name he'd known her by nearly two decades.

"Maggie, I have something else to tell you. Something about Jordan."

She was lost in his embrace, falling the way she

hadn't believed it possible to fall. Still, she forced herself to find his eyes again, to search them for whatever he had to tell her. "Okay . . ."

"I can't be Jordan's special friend anymore." Casey pulled back and studied her face. "Because after all of this, I could never be just a special friend to him."

Megan stared at Casey, not sure what he was saying. Why had he kissed her if he wasn't planning to stay? "You . . . you mean you're leaving us?"

"No, silly." Casey took her hands and kissed her again. "I didn't say that."

"You said you couldn't be his special friend anymore."

"No. I can't be his special friend." Casey locked eyes with her once more, and she felt her heart come to life within her. "Not when all I want . . . is to be his daddy." He let go of one of her hands, reached into his coat pocket, and pulled out something small and shiny. "This . . ." he held it out to her, "belonged to my grandmother."

It was a diamond solitaire, brilliant and set in band of exquisitely etched white gold.

Her gasp was soft, but loud enough for him to hear. He smiled at her, his eyes glazed with tears, and suddenly she knew what was coming, knew he was about to say the words that would change all their lives forever.

And rather than fear it or dread it or doubt it in the least, Megan could hardly wait to say yes. Casey held the ring to her finger and slipped it over her knuckle. Then he kissed her again and spoke the words she was dying to hear.

"Marry me, Maggie Howard. Marry me, and let me love you the way you've always wanted to be loved. Let me be a daddy to Jordan, and let me show you that real love never fails." He hesitated, and she felt tears in her own eyes now. "And together I promise we'll spend forever remembering this moment and believing that yes . . . Christmas miracles really do happen."

Epilogue

IT WAS OCTOBER AGAIN, a year since he'd written the first letter, and now he could hardly wait to write this one. Jordan's parents were in the next room, so he took a piece of paper from his desk drawer—the place where his third-grade homework lay stacked neatly inside. Then he picked his nicest pen from the box on his desk, and steadied his hand over the paper.

Dear God . . .

He smiled at the way his letters looked, then he sucked in a big breath and began again.

I've wanted to write you for a long time, but I wated so I could tell you how good everything is. Plus also my spelling is better so I can write more stuff now. I hope you get this letter, because the daddy you sent me is the best daddy in the whole wide world. And plus something else. My mommy believes in love again. I heard her tell that to Daddy the nite before they got married.

I got to ware my nisest clothes for the wedding, and everyone said they could feel you there with us. I could feel you, too, and not just because it was Valentines Day. Because your kind of love is there every day of the year.

I know it because Daddy says so, and Daddy knows a lot about love.

115

Anyway, I wanted to tell you thanks for reading my letter and making everthing turn out so great. I'll write you again next year. Love, Jordan.

P.S. Thanks for hearing my prayer about a baby sister. Mommy says she'll be here before Christmas.

The Red Gloves Series

Last year, many of you journeyed with me through the pages of my first Warner Christmas story, *Gideon's Gift*. In that book, I shared with you the miracle of a sick little girl and an angry, homeless man, and the gift that changed both their lives forever. And in honor of Gideon's precious gift, at the back of that book I suggested several Red Gloves Projects for you and your friends and families.

In the hundreds of letters you've written me since then, I've heard one theme resonate loudly. You love the idea of the red gloves. Red for Christmas, red for a heart full of love and hope and Christmas miracles.

Red, the color of giving.

And because of that, I've decided to let the red gloves of *Gideon's Gift* play a cameo role in each of my Warner Christmas stories. The Red Gloves Series, we're calling it, and each book will have a new list of Red Gloves Projects. As one of you told me last year, "I bought fifty copies of *Gideon's Gift* to give to everyone I know. My prayer is that we'd see red gloves all around us in the coming years, that they'd grace the hands of the homeless and widowed, the children without parents and parents without hope. So that red gloves would forever be the symbol of Christ's love at Christmas."

In that light, I bring you this year's Red Gloves Projects.

1. Adopt an orphan through WorldVision or another international organization you feel is trustworthy. For usually pennies a day, you can make a difference in the life of at least one child and be to that little boy or girl a Christmas miracle every day of the year. Once you've chosen your child, send him or her a pair of red gloves. Then cut out the child's picture and attach it to a red glove, which can hang in your home all year long.

2. Contact your local branch of Social Services and find out how many children in your area are awaiting families. Make a list of the names of those children and commit along with your friends or family to pray for each of them. Buy gifts for these children, along with several pairs of red gloves, and take the wrapped presents to the local Social Services office. Ask that they be delivered to the children waiting for families.

3. If you're single and able to be more involved, check if your area has an organization that pairs lonely children with willing adults. Make a yearlong commitment to a child, and make your first gift to him or her a pair of red gloves with an explanation that red is the color of giving.

4. Talk to your local public elementary school or contact your church leaders, and locate a needy family in your area. Purchase presents for the

family, and deliver them while wearing red gloves. Adorn the packages with red gloves for each of the children in the family.

I pray this finds you and your family doing well this Christmas, determined to mend broken relationships and let fall the walls that have come between you and those you love. God gave us the greatest gift of all that first Christmas Day.' How much richer we—like Casey Cummins—are when we follow His example and give something back.

Especially something to a child.

Please check out my Web site at www.KarenKingsbury.com for more information about the Red Gloves Projects that have happened since last year. And leave me a note in my guestbook. As always, I'd love to hear from you, and if you have a Red Gloves Project idea you'd like to share with me, please do. I'll add it to my Web site and perhaps suggest it in my Warner Christmas story next year.

Until then, may God's light and life be yours in the coming year.

In His love,

Karen Kingsbury

www.KarenKingsbury.com

An Excerpt from •

Gideon's Gift

THE GIFT THAT CHANGED THEM ALL had led to this: a Christmas wedding.

Nothing could have been more appropriate. Gideon was an angel, after all. Not the haloed, holy kind. But the type that once in a while—when the chance presented itself—made you stare a little harder at her upper back. In case she was sprouting wings.

From his seat in the back of the church, Earl Badgett's tired old eyes grew moist. A Christmas wedding was the only kind for Gideon. Because if ever angels shone it was in December. This was the season when Gideon's gift had mattered most.

Gideon's gift.

A million memories called to him. Had it been thirteen years? Earl stared at the vision she made, surrounded by white satin and lace. The greatest miracle was that Gideon had survived.

He brushed the back of his hand over his damp cheeks. *She actually survived.*

But that wasn't the only miracle.

Earl watched Gideon smile at her father—the glowing, unforgettable smile of a young woman on the brink of becoming. The two of them linked arms and began a graceful walk down the aisle. It was a simple wedding, really. A church full of family and friends, there to witness a most tender moment for a girl who deserved it more than any other. A girl whose love, whose very presence, lit the room and caused people to feel grateful for one reason alone: They had been given the privilege of knowing Gideon Mercer. God had lent her a little while longer to the mere mortals who made up her world. And in that they were all blessed.

Gideon and her father were halfway down the aisle when it happened. Gideon hesitated, glanced over her shoulder, and found Earl. Her eyes had that haunting look that spoke straight to his soul, the same as they always had. They shared the briefest smile, a smile that told him he wasn't the only one. She, too, was remembering the miracle of that Christmas.

The corners of Earl's mouth worked their way up his worn face. You did it, angel. You got your dream. His heart danced with joy. It was all he could do to stay seated, when everything in him wanted to stand and cheer.

Go get 'em, Gideon!

As they rarely did anymore, the memories came like long lost friends. Filling Earl's mind, flooding his senses, linking hands with his heart and leading him back. Back thirteen years to that wondrous time when heaven orchestrated an event no less miraculous than Christmas itself. An event that changed both their lives.

An event that saved them.

Time flew . . . back to the winter when Earl first met Gideon Mercer.

Chapter One

THE RED GLOVES were all that mattered. If living on the streets of Portland was a prison, the red gloves were the key. The key that— for a few brief hours—set him free from the lingering stench and hopeless isolation, free from the relentless rain and the tarp-covered shanty.

The key that freed him to relive the life he'd once had. A life he could never have again.

Something about the red gloves took him back and made it all real—their voices, their touch, their warmth as they sat with him around the dinner table each night. Their love. It was as though he'd never lost a bit of it.

As long as he wore the gloves.

Otherwise, the prison would have been unbearable. Because the truth was Earl had lost everything. His life, his hope, his will to live. But when he slipped on the gloves . . . Ah, when he felt the finely knit wool surround his fingers, Earl still had the one thing that mattered. He still had a family. If only for a few dark hours.

It was the first of November, and the gloves were put away, hidden in the lining of his damp parka. Earl never wore them until after dinner, when he was tucked beneath his plastic roof, anxious to rid himself of another day. He would've loved to wear them all the time, but he didn't dare. They were nice gloves. Handmade. The kind most street people would snatch from a corpse.

Dead or alive, Earl had no intention of losing them.

He shuffled along Martin Luther King Boulevard,

staring at the faces that sped past him. He was invisible to them. Completely invisible. He'd figured that much out his first year on the streets. Oh, once in a while they'd toss him a quarter or shout at him: "Get a job, old man!" or "Go back to California!"

But mostly they just ignored him.

The people who passed him were still in the race, still making decisions and meeting deadlines, still believing it could never happen to them. They carried themselves with a sense of self-reliance—a certainty that they were somehow better than him. For most of them, Earl was little more than a nuisance. An unsightly blemish on the streets of their nice city.

Rain began to fall. Small, icy droplets found their way through his hooded parka and danced across his balding head. He didn't mind. He was used to the rain; it fit his mood. The longer he was on the street the more true that became.

He moved along.

"Big Earl!"

The slurred words carried over the traffic. Earl looked up. A black man was weaving along the opposite sidewalk, shouting and waving a bottle of Crown Royal. He was headed for the same place as Earl: the mission.

Rain or shine, there were meals at the mission. All the street people knew it. Earl had seen the black man there a hundred times before, but he couldn't remember his name. Couldn't remember most of their names. They didn't matter to him. Nothing did. Nothing except the red gloves.

The black man waved the bottle again and shot him a toothless grin. "God loves ya, Big Earl!"

Earl looked away. "Leave me alone," he muttered, and pulled his parka tighter around his neck and face.

124

The mission director had given him the coat two years ago. It had served its purpose. The dark-green nylon was brown now, putrid-smelling and sticky with dirt. Earl's whiskers caught in the fibers and made his face itch.

He couldn't remember the last time he'd shaved.

Across the street the black man gave up. He raised his bottle to a group of three animated women with fancy clothes and new umbrellas. "Dinner bell's a callin' me home, ladies!"

The women stopped chatting and formed a tight, nervous cluster. They squeezed by the man, creating as much distance between them as they could. After they'd passed, the black man raised his bottle again. "God loves ya!"

The mission was two blocks up on the right. Behind him, Earl could hear the black man singing, his words running together like gutter water. Earl's cool response hadn't bothered him at all.

"Amazing grace, how sweet da sound . . ."

Earl narrowed his gaze. Street people wore thick skins. Layers, Earl called it—years of living so far deep inside yourself, nothing could really touch you. Not the weather, not the nervous stares from passersby, not the callous comments from the occasional motorist.

And certainly not anything another street person might say or do.

The mission doors were open. A hapless stream of people mingled among the regulars. Earl rolled his eyes and stared at his boots. When temperatures dropped below fifty, indigents flooded the place. The regulars could barely get a table.

He squeezed his way past the milling newcomers, all of them trying to figure out where the line started and the quickest way to get a hot plate. Up ahead were two empty-eyed drifters—young guys with long hair and years of drug use written on their faces. Earl slid between them, grabbed a plate of food, and headed for his table, a forgotten two-seater off by itself in the far corner of the room.

"Hey, Earl."

He looked up and saw D.J. Grange, mission director for the past decade. The man was bundled in his red-plaid jacket, same as always. His eyes were blue. Too blue. And piercing. As though he could see things Earl didn't tell anyone. D.J. was always talking God this and God that. It was amazing, really. After all these years, D.J. still didn't get it.

Earl looked back down at his plate. "I don't come for a sermon. You know that," he mumbled into his instant mashed potatoes.

"We got people praying, Earl." D.J. gripped the nearest chair and leaned closer. Earl could feel the man's smile without looking. "Any requests? Just between us?"

"Yes." Earl set his fork down and shot D.J. the hardest look he could muster. "Leave me alone."

"Fine." D.J. grinned like a shopping-mall Santa Claus. "Let me know if you change your mind." Still smiling, he moved on to the next table.

There was one other chair at Earl's table, but no one took it. There was an unspoken code among street people—sober ones, anyway: "Eyes cast down, don't come around." Earl kept his eyes on his plate, and on this night the code worked. The others would rather stand than share a meal with a man who needed his space.

Besides his appearance would easily detract even the most hardened street people. He didn't look in the mir-

126

ror often, but when he did, he understood why they kept their distance. It wasn't his scraggly, gray hair or the foul-smelling parka. It was his eyes.

Cold, dead eyes.

The only time he figured his eyes might possibly show signs of life or loneliness was at night. When he wore the red gloves. But then, no one ever saw his eyes during those hours.

He finished his plate, pushed back from the table and headed for the exit. D.J. watched him go, standing guard at the front of the food line. "See you tomorrow, Earl." He waved big. "I'll be praying for you."

Earl didn't turn around. He walked hard and fast out the door into the dark, rainy night. It was colder than before. It worried him a little. Some years, when the first cold night had hit, another street person had swiped his bed or taken off with his tarp. His current tarp hung like a curtain across the outside wall of his home. It was easily the most important part of his physical survival. Small wonder they were taken so often.

He narrowed his eyes and picked up his pace. His back hurt and he felt more miserable than usual. He was anxious for sleep, anxious to shut out the world and everything bad about it.

Anxious for the red gloves.

He'd spent this day like every other day, wandering the alleyways and staring at his feet. He always took his meals at the mission and waited. For sundown, for sleep, for death. Years ago, when he'd first hit the streets, his emotions had been closer to the surface. Sorrow and grief and guilt, fear and loneliness and anxiety. Hourly these would seize him, strangling his battered heart like a vice grip.

But each day on the streets had built in him another

layer, separating him from everything he'd ever felt, everything about the man he used to be and the life he used to lead. His emotions were buried deep now, and Earl was sure they'd never surface again. He was a shell—a meaningless, unfeeling shell.

His existence was centered in nothingness and nightfall.

He rounded the corner and through the wet darkness he saw his home. It was barely noticeable, tucked beneath an old wrought-iron stairwell deep in the heart of a forgotten alley. Hanging from seven rusty bolts along the underside of the stairs was the plastic tarp. He lifted the bottom of it off the ground and crawled inside. No matter how wet it was, rain almost never found its way beyond the tarp. His pillow and pile of old blankets were still dry.

He'd been waiting for this moment all day.

His fingers found the zipper in the lining of his parka and lowered it several inches. He tucked his hand inside and found them, right where he'd left them this morning. As soon as he made contact with the soft wool, the layers began to fall away, exposing what was left of his heart.

Carefully he pulled the gloves out and slipped them onto his fingers, one at a time. He stared at them, studied them, remembering the hands that had knit them a lifetime ago. Then he did something that had become part of his routine, something he did every night at this time. He brought his hands to his face and kissed first one woolen palm and then the other.

"Good night, girls." He muttered the words out loud. Then he lay down and covered himself with the tattered blankets. When he was buried far beneath, when the warmth of his body had served to sufficiently warm the place where he slept, he laced his gloved fingers together and drifted off to sleep.

The next morning he was still half given to a wonderful dream when he felt rain on his face. Rain and a stream of light much brighter than usual. With eyes closed, he turned his head from side to side. What was it? Where was the water coming from and why wasn't his tarp working?

He rubbed his fingers together—

—and sat straight up.

"No!" His voice ricocheted off the brick walls of the empty alley.

"Noooo!" He stood up and yelled as loudly as he could—a gut-wrenching, painful cry of the type he hadn't uttered since that awful afternoon five years ago.

His head was spinning. He grabbed at his hair, pulled it until his scalp hurt. It wasn't possible. Yet . . .

He'd been robbed. In the middle of the night someone had found him sleeping and taken most of what made up his home. His tarp was gone. Most of his blankets, too.

But that wasn't all. They had stolen everything left of his will to live, everything he had to look forward to. Nothing this bad had happened to him since he took to the streets. He shook his head in absolute misery as a driving rain pelted his skin, washing away all that remained of his sleep.

He stared at his hands, his body trembling. The thing he'd feared most of all had finally happened.

The red gloves were gone

Dear Reader:

I hope you enjoyed reading this Large Print book. If you are interested in reading other Beeler Large Print titles, ask your librarian or write to me at:

Thomas T. Beeler, *Publisher*
Post Office Box 310
Rollinsford, New Hampshire 03869-0310

You can also call me at 1-800-818-7574 and I will send you my latest catalogue.

Traci Wason and I choose the titles I publish in Large Print. Our aim is to provide good books by outstanding authors—books we both enjoyed reading and liked well enough to want to share. We warmly welcome any suggestions for new titles and authors.

Sincerely,